RETURN TO EVIL

A DCI HARRY MCNEIL NOVEL

JOHN CARSON

FRANK MILLER SERIES

RETURN TO EVIL

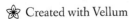 Created with Vellum

To the memory of the real Harry McNeil.

My wife's uncle.

Cheryl, Cindy and Penny's dad.

A true gentleman.

ONE

MAY 1999

Jill entered through the side gate of the cemetery and hurried along the track that ran parallel to the road behind the high wall. The old caretaker's house was over on the left, but she took a fork in the road and went right. There was a small hill here, which blocked the view of the house.

Their meeting point.

She slowed down and started to cry.

Then a figure stepped out from behind a large gravestone.

She caught her breath and jumped. Then she recognised him. Her boyfriend.

'Oh, thank God you came,' she said, running to him and throwing her arms around his neck.

'Of course I came.'

It was dark now. Spits of rain fell through the canopy of trees. Most people would be scared to come into a cemetery after dark, but Jill found it peaceful and comforting. *You didn't have to fear the dead in here* she had told a friend.

Her boyfriend's arms felt good around her. 'Did you tell your wife about us?' she said. Then pulled back to look him in the eyes.

'Not yet. I promise I will. The timing has to be just right.'

'I know. I understand. I can't wait until we're a family.'

'It's going to happen soon.' He held her close again.

Then they parted and she stood looking at him. 'I told my dad I'm pregnant.'

'You did what?' A look of anger passed over his face.

'Please don't be angry. He was drinking again. My mother is God knows where, so I just blurted it out. I told him we're going to go away together.'

'Jesus. These things take time to plan. We can't just rush into it. It's called *adulting*. We don't want it to go pear-shaped.'

'Don't talk to me like I'm a child.'

'You're fifteen. You *are* a child.'

'Don't talk like that! I'm going to be your wife. When I'm old enough, we can get married. We'll have our baby.'

They both heard the shouting at the same time.

Jill! Where are you?

'Oh my God. He must have followed me.' The shouting got closer, then they saw the torchlight cutting through the darkness.

'He's coming. He knows we hang out at the old house here.'

'Stay calm,' her boyfriend said. 'Just tell him you're meeting a friend here and you'll be back home soon.' He slipped away into the darkness, out of sight behind a large gravestone.

'Are you still there?' she whispered.

'Yes. Stay calm. I'll be right here.'

Jill! Then the light picked out her face and blinded her.

'There you are. What are you doing here?'

'Just go home. You shouldn't be here.'

'*I* shouldn't be here? You're the one who should be home, waiting to explain to your mother!' He was swaying and Jill could smell the drink on him.

'You're drunk. Go home.'

'You're coming with me.' He reached out and grabbed her arm, but she pulled away, her nails catching his arm.

'You're not my real dad!' she spat.

'Jesus. You listen to me; you get home right now!' He stepped forward and tripped, falling forward and banging his head on a gravestone. He lay unconscious.

Jill's boyfriend stepped out from behind the grave.

'I think he's dead,' she said, putting a hand to her mouth.

The boyfriend reached down and felt her dad's neck for a pulse. 'He's alive. He's just out cold.'

'Thank God.' She looked at the love of her life and thought how much she loved him. Then she looked down at the prone figure of her father.

She didn't see her boyfriend come up behind her with the little stone vase, didn't see him swing it. All she felt was a sharp pain on the back of her head. The whole world swam in front of her eyes and she couldn't stand straight, then her legs buckled. She fell close to her father.

She couldn't speak, then she felt the hands under her armpits and she was being dragged, away from her father. Now she was lying sideways across the grave. What was going on?

Where was her boyfriend?

She saw the hands on the gravestone above her; wanted to move but couldn't. Then she heard a grunt of exertion.

Her last thought before she died was, *The baby!*

Then it was all over.

TWO

PRESENT DAY

'Slow it down a bit, pal. My head's about to explode,' Blinky said from the passenger seat of the Transit tipper truck.

'If you toss your bag in here, you'll be cleaning it mind,' Joe *Rats* Ratcliffe said. He slowed the work truck down as it bounced into the cemetery. The ride-on lawnmower and other grounds-keeping tools rattled about in the back of the trailer and in the bed of the truck.

'I should have taken your advice last night and capped it at six pints. Never again.'

'I told you but, oh no, you knew best.' Rats drove the small truck straight ahead. All the film crew's vehicles were parked up on the left, round the side of the cottage; caravans, vans, big production vehicles that looked like converted coaches. All the ancillary things that went with making a TV show.

'There's Honey Summers over there,' Rats said, pointing. Blinky was in the back of the cab, groaning.

'I don't know what the fuss is all about with that one.'

'What? Are you daft? She's one of the hottest actresses on TV right now. I for one can't wait to see this show when they finish it.' He swerved away from a gravestone as he put his eyes back in. They were on the gravel track that led down into the lower part of the cemetery.

'It's not going to be on TV until next year,' Blinky said. 'And slow it down. It feels like I'm on a roller coaster.'

'Look at you. What a state. I don't want you skiving off and leaving me to do all the work.'

'I'll be fine. I have my flask with me. Filled with black coffee.'

Blinky groaned again as the truck stopped.

'You want to use the strimmer first while I use the lawnmower?' Rats said.

'Is this the face of somebody who gives a toss?'

'Come on, get up. The fresh air will do you good.'

Rats jumped out and opened the back door where

Blinky was trying to get up. 'That's it boy, up and at 'em!' Rats shouted.

'Jesus. I'm going to run you over with that mower when it's my turn.'

Rats laughed and clapped his friend on the shoulder as Blinky got out and stood on shaky legs.

'Jesus, what's that smell?' Rats said.

'It's not me.' Blinky looked around.

'I hope you brought a spare pair of skids,' Rats said, walking round the truck. Then he stopped and put an arm out as his friend came to join him.

'What's wrong, Rats? You see a ghost or something?'

'Look. There's a lassie there. Lying on the grass.'

'Is there somebody with her?'

'I know I don't wear glasses like you but my eyesight's not that good that I can see through gravestones.' He looked at his friend and shook his head.

Shoes were hanging off the feet and Rats could see the red toenail polish. Low hanging branches and bushes partially hid the girl's features. A large headstone blocked their view of the girl.

'Do you think there's a couple round there going at it?'

'Have a word. It's just gone ten.'

'Oh, there's opening times for it now, is there?'

Rats looked at his friend and shook his head. 'If

they were going at it, then don't you think the sound of a diesel engine might have made them sit up and take notice?'

'I'm going to have a look.' Blinky walked towards the gravestone, looked round and retched. Then he turned to Rats, wiping his mouth with the back of his hand. 'Call the cops.'

THREE

The sky was overcast now, bringing with it a cold wind. Perfect weather for being in a cemetery.

'Jesus, what a way to go,' Detective Inspector Frank Miller said. 'Just when we think we've seen it all.'

'Nothing surprises me anymore,' Detective Chief Inspector Harry McNeil said, as they stood inside the large forensics tent. 'At least it must have been quick.'

A large gravestone, grey and lichen-covered with age, was lying flat on the top half of the woman. Only her bottom half was showing, the very top of her jeans soaked in blood.

They stepped out into the cold. It had been warmer earlier, but Edinburgh's weather liked to play games.

The forensics team were doing their thing and had

been scouring over the scene all day. They would lift the gravestone soon and give her some dignity.

Miller wasn't wearing an overcoat, thinking he didn't need one when he'd left the house that morning. He was shivering slightly.

'Come and walk with me over here, Frank.'

Harry started walking away from the scene and Miller followed him.

He stopped at a gravestone near the site of the old caretaker's house which had been pulled down in the past few years. Miller stood looking up at a gravestone that sat on an incline. The stone looked like a monument rather than a death marker. The small hill blocked the view of the demolished house.

'What is it about this cemetery, Frank?' Harry said. 'The things that have gone on in here, you would think it's the only cemetery in Edinburgh. Why this place? What draws people here?'

Miller blew his breath out. 'It's such an old place. Whoever designed it made the front of the catacombs look like the front of a castle. It draws you in. Draws the darker side of some people.'

Harry turned to face Miller. He was standing between two gravestones. 'She died here. Jill Thompson. Twenty years ago, this summer. She was fifteen years old. She was found crushed to death under a gravestone. Right where I'm standing. She was murdered and nobody was ever caught.'

'I remember being here, too, but I was only a boy,' Miller said. 'She was just a child, not much older than me.'

'That didn't stop somebody from killing her.'

Both men stood in silence for a moment before Harry spoke.

'You ready for this, Frank?'

Miller looked at him, and thought of a young girl whose life had been ended prematurely in a cold, dark cemetery twenty years ago.

'I've never been more ready.'

'Then let's do it.'

FOUR

FIVE DAYS LATER

Harry McNeil stood looking in the bathroom mirror when his girlfriend came and stood in the doorway.

'Your tie's squint,' Vanessa said, smiling at him.

'My head feels squint.' He fiddled with his tie. 'There should be a law against Monday mornings.'

'I told you to go easy last night. What with it being Sunday and you having to get up early this morning.'

'I was just being sociable. It's all Stan's fault.' McNeil looked again but his tie still looked squint.

'For goodness sake, I have four-year-old's in my nursery who can do a tie better than that.'

'Give one of them a call. Maybe he can come along and do this one for me.'

Vanessa stepped forward and turned him to face her. 'You're going to blame Stan for getting you drunk?' She fiddled around with the tie. 'Anyway, isn't it his retirement party next week?'

'It is, but last night was just the two of us. Stan was giving me some last-minute tips. He'll be showing me the ropes for a couple of weeks until I head the department.'

Vanessa shook her head. 'You've been a copper for over twenty years. A lot of miles under your belt. And you're only forty. I don't think you need tips on being a detective.'

'Easy. Forty in two weeks. Or had you forgotten?'

'No, I haven't forgotten, smarty pants.'

'Harry doesn't feel well and you're playing games,' he said. 'Harry wants sympathy and paracetamol. And more coffee.'

'No, yes and there's some water in the kettle. And while you're at it, tell Harry to get a move on. We don't want him to be late on his first day.'

'First day back on regular duty after being on the ghost squad for four years.'

'I've never heard you call Professional Standards that before.'

'It's just one of the names the others call us. Some-times we have to be like ghosts, appearing when we want to and when we're least expected.'

'It's going to be a big change for you, but let's not forget the C word.'

McNeil raised his eyebrows.

'*Chief,*' Vanessa said. 'Detective *Chief* Inspector Harry McNeil.'

'It does have a certain ring to it.'

'Stan is going to be proud of you.'

'He's a good guy, although he likes a wee drink to himself. I can't keep up with him at times.' They left the bathroom and went through to the kitchen where Harry poured himself anther coffee.

'Didn't Stan drink on duty?' Vanessa said.

'It was something over nothing. I was lead investigator on that. When somebody dropped him in it, he was off duty. They were trying to get back at him.'

'Don't get me wrong, Stan's a nice guy. You two go way back, but it just seems a coincidence that three months after that happened, Stan's retiring.'

'He'd been thinking about it for ages. They needed somebody competent enough to head up the cold case unit, but nobody fit the bill.'

'Until Stan put in a good word for you. You two are as thick as thieves.' She gave him a kiss.

'You're not wired, are you? Recording this conversation, trying to incriminate me?' He smiled but something in the way she'd said it had suddenly put him on guard.

'Yeah, so don't try and make a run for it. The building's surrounded.' She laughed. 'I'm so glad you got the promotion. And you just have to walk down the hill and you're right at HQ.' She scuttled about getting her things together. 'See you at dinner. No, wait; it's parents' evening. I won't be home until later.'

'You own the nursery, why can't you just let the teachers do it?'

She smiled a sad smile and shook her head. 'I wish. But don't worry, there are some microwave dinners in the freezer. You won't starve. And remember to give Frank a call.'

She blew him a kiss and left her house.

Remember to give Frank a call. DI Frank Miller. Harry was still renting Frank's flat around the corner, the one Frank had owned with his first wife, Carol, who was now deceased.

He spread out his copy of the morning paper, *The Caledonian*, and started reading through it, but his mind wasn't on that day's news.

Vanessa's flat was in Learmonth looking down the hill to the Comely Bank bowling club. Looking down towards the flat he rented, which also overlooked the bowling club.

The club was where they had met. A birthday party was being held there and they had been introduced. That had been almost eighteen months ago.

They spent most nights at her place, but sometimes Harry wanted the solitude of his own apartment. Now Vanessa had talked about him moving in permanently and she had asked him to talk to Frank about giving up the flat.

He knew he should be thankful for having Vanessa in his life, but it was just a big step.

His mobile phone rang. It was Stan.

'Harry! I just wanted to call and wish you the best of luck.'

'Thanks, Stan, but you did that last night. And how are you not lying in bed with your head over the side, trying not to choke on your own vomit?'

Stan laughed. 'Years more experience than you, laddie. I've already had a big fry-up and I'm meeting my mucker tonight for a sesh. Sorry I'm not going to be there to show you around, but they have me going to talk to somebody in HR about my upcoming retirement. Waste of time, if you ask me, but rules are rules I suppose.'

'Don't worry about it. I'm sure one of the others can show me around.'

'Just remember what I told you about them.' There was silence for a moment. 'You don't fancy coming along for a pint tonight, do you?'

Harry hesitated for a moment.

'It's okay if you're busy,' Stan said.

'No, it's fine. Vanessa is working late anyway.'

'Great. *Diamonds* at eight?'

'I'll be there.'

'Good man.'

Harry disconnected the call. Another sesh with Stan. Vanessa would lecture him again, no doubt. He'd stay over at his own place tonight. Maybe go into work tomorrow without a tie. Or buy a clip-on.

He didn't want to get dragged out to the pub with Stan every night, but he had few friends as it was. The friends he had had on the force at one time now gave him excuses when he wanted to meet up. Four years in Standards and they treated him like he was the Grim Reaper.

Nobody could blame them, least of all McNeil.

Outside, summer was knocking on the door. He unlocked his car and got in. It was a Honda CR-V. It had been his wife's, but she had let him have it in the divorce settlement. She had been quite happy to take the house, but the thing that's value was going rapidly in the opposite direction, he could have. He still told people it was his wife's, in case they wondered why he was driving a girl's car. *Mine is in the garage*, he would tell them.

Morag had got the house, sold it, and moved with their son, Chance, to Fife, where her family lived. That had been after the argument which led to her brother coming across and clocking him one. If it hadn't been for the can of pepper spray and his extendable baton, McNeil might have been in a worse state.

It had ended without any charges, thanks to McNeil getting the upper hand.

Chance was fifteen now, Harry thought as he pulled out from the kerb. This was going to be a five-minute drive down to Fettes HQ, if he got through the green light first time. Which he did. Walk there, indeed. *Do I look like the sort of bloke who likes to exercise?*

Then he was pulling into the car park off Fettes Avenue, behind the Waitrose store.

It had been a long time since he had set foot in this building. It looked like an office block from the seventies that had somehow missed the wrecking ball. No doubt some developer one day would be drooling over it, especially since the neighbour across the road was Fettes College, a prestige school. The same one that Tony Blair had gone to, but Harry didn't think that would hold bragging rights these days.

He passed through security and headed upstairs to the cold case offices. And when he stepped into the incident room, there was a giant of a man about to throw a computer out the window.

FIVE

'When they said the computers use Windows, I don't think that's what they had in mind,' Harry said, standing looking at the big man.

He turned to Harry. 'Oh, hi, boss.' The man grinned and put the old monitor down on a desk. 'I was just telling the others that you can use anything to work out with.'

'It's all fun and games until somebody loses an eye,' Harry replied.

'Even a couple of cans of beans could get your arms started.' He nodded vaguely in the direction of Harry's biceps, an unspoken insinuation that Harry still paid the gym membership but didn't frequent the place.

'Well, I've had my beans for the day. The coffee kind.' Maybe he'd start walking to work after all.

'Ignore him, boss,' a young woman said, getting up

from behind her desk. The other faces in the incident room looked at her.

'I'm DS Alexis Maxwell. Everybody calls me Alex. Except him.' She nodded over to the big man. 'DC Simon Gregg. Everybody calls him *Simple*, except his mum.'

'Welcome, boss.' Gregg shook Harry's hand, then the phone rang on Alex's desk. She answered it, spoke and hung up again.

'And we call her *Alexa*, like that Amazon woman. *Alexa, answer the phone*, that sort of thing.' Gregg turned to Alex. 'Who was on the phone?'

'It was the village again. They're still looking for their idiot. I told them you were busy.'

Gregg made a face.

Harry reminded himself to tell Stan at the pub that night, that a better heads-up would have been appreciated.

He looked at the others.

'This is DI Karen Shiels,' Alex said.

Harry nodded to the woman, who looked to be in her forties. She gave a grim smile back.

'These two gentlemen are retired detectives, brought back to help out the team. George Carr and Willie Young,' Alex said.

'It's a pleasure, gentlemen,' Harry said, and the two older men nodded to him. He looked around at them all, sure they knew in advance who he was, but he didn't want any ambiguity.

'My name is DCI Harry McNeil. I spent the last four years in Professional Standards. I haven't investigated any of you, as that would have precluded me from heading this department, so I don't know any of you personally, but I hope to get to know you better. Any questions?'

None.

'If any of you have a problem with me being in Standards, speak up now or forever hold your peace.' He looked around at them each in turn, but none of them said a word.

'Good. I now pronounce us boss and team. I will be working alongside DCI Weaver for a couple of weeks until he retires, then I take over the reins. I need another coffee and then we can sit down and go over the case. DCI Weaver told me there was a case ready to go, so let me get some caffeine and we can get started.' He turned to Alex. 'Can you show me where the canteen is?'

'We have a kettle,' Gregg said.

Harry raised his eyes at Alex.

'I'm sure the boss doesn't want to drink our coffee before putting money in the kitty,' she said, walking out of the incident room, Harry following.

'I had a read of your profiles last week,' he said as

they made their way downstairs. 'It didn't go into details as to why you're here. All the files told me was your names, age, rank and where you were stationed before you came here.'

'DCI Weaver didn't tell you about us?' Alex replied, scepticism in her voice.

'He was going to, but I told him I wanted to get the first impression for myself.' They walked towards the canteen. 'So, what's your story?'

She cleared her throat as they went through the door and stood in line for breakfast. 'I punched a prisoner. He was handcuffed, but he headbutted me. As I bent forward, he tried to bring his cuffed hands down on my neck, according to witnesses, but I knew I was in trouble. So I punched him hard between the legs.'

'Seems fair enough to me,' he replied as they shuffled along the queue.

'He was the Lord Provost's son.' Alex ordered two bacon rolls, one to be bagged. 'One for the Jolly Green Giant,' she explained. 'Six foot six and acts like he's five, but we love him.'

'I can see how he could come in handy if we need a door taken down quickly. We can use him as a battering ram.'

'He's a sweetheart.'

Harry ordered a bacon roll as well, and they took them and ordered two coffees. When they reached the cash register, Harry paid. 'Mark this day on your calendar. The boss is not always going to be this generous.'

'Duly noted,' she said, smiling. 'You want to sit at a table?'

'What about Gregg's roll? It'll get cold.'

'That doesn't matter. I've seen him eat worse.'

They caught an empty table, Harry not wanting to ask what worse things the DC had eaten.

'DCI Weaver said I had to sit down with you all, one by one, and get the lowdown on why you're here, in the cold case unit, but that's a waste of time,' Harry said. 'That's why I've delegated you. If you're comfortable with that.' He took a bite out of his bacon roll. He didn't want to put ketchup on it, just in case it squirted out on his tie. God forbid he would have to put another one on. Maybe switching to a bow tie in future would be the way to go.

'Of course I am,' She took a bite out of her own roll, washing it down with coffee. 'Look at us, like we're out on a first date. And you paying for the meal. You're going to give me a reputation, sir.'

'Your reputation precedes you,' Harry answered. 'What did Weaver have you call him?'

'Stan, or boss. Whatever we were comfortable with. Except in front of other officers, then it was boss, or DCI Weaver. What do you want us to call you, Harry?'

'Cheeky. But Harry is fine. Same rules apply though.'

She grinned. 'Of course.'

'Now start off by telling me about yourself.' He ate and drank and listened.

'When I made it to detective sergeant, I thought I was heading in the right direction, promotion wise, until the Lord Provost incident. Just my luck, he was good friends with the Edinburgh commander. Not Jeni Bridge, her predecessor. I was transferred to the cold case unit, which I thought was just for older detectives waiting out their time 'til retirement. Seems I was wrong.'

'Perceptions can be deceiving at times. I was Shanghaied into Standards, and I didn't think it would be too bad, at first. Turns out, you get treated like you're the one caught with the can of petrol after the orphanage was burnt down. But tell me more.'

Alex nodded. 'I was stationed at the West End. Before I got sent here, two years ago. I'm twenty-nine, been in the force since I was eighteen. I was in a long-term relationship until a year ago. It didn't work out. We were engaged to be married, had bought a house together, but after we split up, we sold the house and now I've bought a flat in the Stockbridge Colonies—'

Harry held up a hand. 'We've gone a little bit off

topic. This is not your pitch for Tinder.' He smiled at her red face.

'I'm pulling a beamer here, aren't I?' she said.

'Yes, but I'm pretending not to notice.'

'Right, Stuart Gregg. Twenty-five. He left his post on a surveillance job, and the person he was supposed to be looking out for left and they couldn't find him. The same guy went on to rob a bank and he stabbed two workers.'

'I hope he had a good excuse.'

'He did. He got a call saying his wife and baby daughter had been in a car accident.'

'Were they okay?'

'They were both dead on arrival at the Royal.'

'Jesus.' Harry looked at her. 'And they put him here as punishment?'

'Yes,' Alex replied. 'The brilliant commander.'

'What's the deal with Karen?' Harry asked, finishing his own roll.

'She had a breakdown. She had reported a senior officer for sexual assault. Nobody listened. She got into an altercation with the officer at the police club. She had gone there with some friends. The officer was in there. He cornered her and she hit him. In self-defence, but the commander didn't see it that way. That was a year ago.'

'You're telling me this officer attacked a junior officer, and now Karen is here? What happened to the senior guy?'

'Nothing.'

'As a former investigator, that hacks me off, let me tell you,' Harry said.

'It happens.' Alex finished her roll.

'Not to my team it doesn't. Nobody better put a hand on anybody else. You have me on your side now.'

'I appreciate that, sir.'

'And I know about the two older guys in the office. Weaver did tell me about *them*. A couple of good guys.'

'They have a wealth of experience,' she said, as they got up and made their way upstairs.

'Experience counts for a lot,' Harry said as they got back to the squad room. Gregg now had Willie Young above his head.

'Then you would just slam the bastard down on the deck and kick him right in the you-know-what.'

'Mother of God,' Harry said, shaking his head. 'Please tell me this isn't a daily occurrence.'

Gregg put the older man down. 'Just showing them a bit of self-defence, boss,' he said, grinning.

'Next time the village is on the phone, tell them to come and collect him,' Harry said.

'Your office is over there, sir,' George Carr pointed towards a door.

'Thanks. I'm also going to take a desk out here.

There seem to be a few spare.'

They looked at each other. 'That's not what DCI Weaver does,' Young said, looking ruffled after his bit of audience participation.

'Well, now I'm going to be in charge, so I think I'll have a desk out here as well. That way, I'll hear what you're saying behind my back, but as it won't be behind my back. I won't have to hear it second-hand in the canteen.'

Alex smiled. 'Now why would you go and spoil all the fun?'

Harry sat down at an empty desk. 'Somebody go and get the file, so we can start work.'

'It's not that easy, sir,' Carr said. 'Things have changed. Commander Bridge was on the phone. This one is going to be different.'

'In what way?' Harry asked.

'It has similarities to the death that occurred last Wednesday. I assume you heard about it?'

'The girl in the cemetery? Yes, I heard about it.'

'She was killed in the same way as a girl almost twenty years ago.'

Harry looked at the others. 'Why do they think they're linked?'

'You'll be liaising with DI Frank Miller, sir. He'll tell you. They want you and Alex at the mortuary. Right away.'

SIX

Miller was at the mortuary with DS Steffi Walker. 'What happened to you?' he asked her, looking at the bruise round her eye.

'I know, I'm a clumsy cow. I tripped on the cat and fell into the ironing board.'

'Might be an idea to get Peter to iron his own shirts, now that he's moved in with you.'

'He does. He told me he ironed his shirts when he had his own place.'

Miller smiled. 'Maybe add a little bit more water to your drink?'

'I wish.'

Harry McNeil walked in with Alex, and Miller turned towards him.

'Good morning, sir,' Miller said.

'Good morning. This is DS Alex Maxwell.'

'DS Steffi Walker. We've been told that we're working on this case together. This is why we're all here,' Miller explained.

'Okay. Sounds good.'

'Good morning,' Professor Leo Chester said as he came into the PM suite.

'Good morning,' they replied like schoolchildren.

Kate Murphy and Jake Dagger came in behind the professor and they exchanged pleasantries.

'I asked for you to attend here today because there is news; the girl, Trisha Cornwall, was murdered and that changes everything,' Chester said.

'What are you marking as the cause of death?' Harry asked.

'The gravestone was estimated to be twenty-two stone,' Kate said. 'It did horrific damage to her insides but we did our best to measure her height and she was around five six. Her features were completely deformed, as you can imagine.'

The detectives agreed they could imagine.

'We've been working over the past few days to try and reconstruct as much of her as possible, and we found a round hole in the back of her skull,' Jake Dagger said. 'Not immediately apparent, but when we put the skull together, it was there. It looks like she was hit by something blunt and round, like a hammer. Nothing on the gravestone could have caused that damage, so it had to have been inflicted before it was pushed over on her. Cause of death, blunt force trauma.'

'Seems a bit like overkill,' Harry said.

'We've all heard of psychos who stab somebody seventy times in a fit of rage,' Alex said.

'That seems to be the case here,' Miller agreed. He turned to Harry. 'Commander Bridge will want a rundown of things. I'll meet you up at the station, sir?'

'Okay. See you up there.'

They left by the back door and drove up to the station further up the Royal Mile.

'You're quiet today, Steffi. Usually we can't get you to shut up.'

'I had a busy weekend, sir. Just doing things around the house. And I had a few drinks with Peter since he had the weekend off.'

'Do you ever go down to the police club?'

She looked at him. Such a sad look on her face, he thought. 'No. We don't go there. Sometimes we go out with some of his bus driving colleagues.'

Steffi said nothing as Miller pulled the car into the rear car park, driving through the vennel under the old building.

Alex pulled her car in and parked next to him.

DS Andy Watt was standing outside talking to one

of the uniforms. 'Here they come, the back-shift,' he said as Miller and Steffi got out of the car.

'Fuck off, Andy,' Steffi said, brushing past him and going through the back door.

Watt looked at Miller. 'I'm taking that bottle of aftershave back. The saleswoman said it would attract women like bees to honey, not make them tell you to fuck off. What a swizz.'

'Some men just have it naturally, Andy.' It was warmer than the weekend had been, the sun coming out in a blue sky.

'Seriously, boss, what's wrong with her? She's always up for a bit of banter. And what's with the eye?'

'She said she tripped over her cat and hit the ironing board.'

Watt gave Miller a look. 'She doesn't have a cat.'

'Maybe she got one. Maybe Peter had one and took it with him.'

'And I ride a unicorn to work.'

They started walking to the back door. 'Just don't mention I told you.'

'You got it.'

'This is DCI McNeil, and DS Alex Maxwell. They're working on the gravestone case,' Miller said.

They went up to the investigation suite on the fourth floor and were directed along to one of the conference rooms.

Detective Superintendent Percy Purcell was head of CID. He was waiting with Edinburgh Division Commander, Jeni Bridge.

'Sit down, everybody,' Jeni Bridge said. There was a jug of water in the middle of the conference table with glasses around it.

'DCI McNeil and DS Maxwell are from the cold case unit,' Jeni said, 'and I've invited them along here today because I was in a meeting at the Crown Office last week, discussing the body that was found in Warriston cemetery on Wednesday morning.' She looked at Harry. 'I was informed by Professor Chester at the mortuary that it's now officially murder. Blunt force trauma to the back of the head. The woman was in quite a mess and it took a few days to reconstruct her skull.'

Purcell leaned forward. 'As you are all aware, MIT are called out to any scene like last Friday's discovery, as a matter of course. Just in case. Now we've had confirmation, we can look at this case through a different set of goggles.

'First of all, the victim's name is Trisha Cornwall. She comes from down south and her next of kin have been informed. The Metropolitan Police are talking to the family to get some background. But the reason you're here, DCI McNeil, is because of the similar case to this one from twenty years ago. You'll be lead investigator on this case, with DI Miller riding shotgun. You'll be working with DCI Weaver in your cold case unit.'

Harry looked at him. 'The only information I was given this morning was that we would be working with DI Miller. My team member didn't go into any details of the case.'

'It concerns the unsolved murder of a young teenage girl, back in July 1999. Jill Thompson. Have any of the older members of the team heard of this case?' Jeni asked.

'I have,' Harry said. 'I was in uniform. I hadn't been on the force long.'

'I have,' Miller said. All eyes were now on him and he felt like he was on a game show. 'I was brought up in Warriston Road. The cemetery was our playground during the summer holidays. We used to play football there and ride our bikes about in safety. We watched them filming the first *God Complex*. I was ten at the time.'

'Did you know the victim?'

'No. I mean, she came to our street with her friends, and they would hang out near the trailers that the TV stars stayed in between filming. I knew *of* her, but me and my friends didn't hang out with them. She stayed along the other end of Warriston Road.' He looked at some of the others. 'For those of you who don't know the area, Warriston Road is split into two;

there are allotments and the crematorium between the two parts. Jill lived in the Ferry Road end. I lived in the St Mark's Park end.'

Jeni nodded then turned to Purcell. 'If you could get everybody up to speed.'

'Certainly.' He opened the folder that was sitting on the table in front of him, extracting a sheaf of papers, which were passed around. Crime scene photos from back in the day.

It was hot and stuffy in the room. Miller reached over and poured himself a glass of water. Looked down at the gravestone lying on top of the girl. From 1999. It could have been the same scene from a couple of days ago.

When everybody had copies, Purcell started reading. 'But as for our original victim; Jill was fifteen at the time of her death, and three months pregnant.'

Harry looked at the photos of the young girl. She was pretty, with a nice smile, and he could see why a young man might be interested in her. Or some, perverted, older men.

'Known boyfriend?' he asked.

'Yes. There was talk of a boyfriend, and she had written about him in a diary. That means nothing, of course, but somebody had to have got her pregnant.'

'Who found her?' one of the detectives asked.

'There was a young man who lived in the street. A

loner. No girlfriend, no real friends. He was a teenager, around the same age as Jill.' Purcell looked at Miller again.

Miller nodded. 'I knew him. Graham Balfour. He would hang out with me and my pals despite being a bit older. I think he was around fourteen at the time. A bit weird.'

'We took the liberty of doing some preliminaries on this. Balfour still lives there, according to the voters' roll,' Purcell said.

'Does he have a record?' Harry asked.

'He's a registered sex offender. Pissing in public. But that's all,' Jeni said.

'Times have certainly changed,' Purcell said. 'Drunks all over Edinburgh would use a hedge after being in the boozer and nobody said a word.'

They were all looking at him.

'I'm not condoning, like.'

'Anyway,' Jeni continued, 'I would like Miller and his team to go and talk to the film crew who are back today. There was a security guard on duty on Wednesday, but he saw nothing and heard nothing. And McNeil can take DS Maxwell and go through the old murder with DCI Weaver and the rest of his team.' She looked at Harry. 'You will both work with Miller here at the High Street until told otherwise.'

'Yes, ma'am.'

'Any other questions?'

'Is there DNA from the first crime scene?' Miller asked.

'Yes. It's being taken to the labs. DNA has moved on quite a bit in twenty years, so they'll do their thing.'

Harry put a finger up. 'How did they come to the conclusion that Jill Thompson was murdered?'

'By the position of the body,' Purcell said. 'And the height of the gravestone. Distance, her weight, and the weight of the stone. Children have been killed by climbing onto gravestones which have then toppled over, but we did some research last week, and all the victims in the UK were small children. When the stones toppled, their feet were off the ground, so it was harder for them to jump clear. And the stones were bigger than them so even when they fell back, the stone was big enough to cover most of their body. Jill's body was in a completely different position than if she'd been climbing on it. Therefore, it was determined that somebody pushed it on top of her.'

'No sign of a hole in her skull like this new victim?'

'Nothing was in the pathology report.'

'Right,' Jeni said, 'Miller, you and DS Walker are going over to interrupt filming in the cemetery. McNeil, you and DS Maxwell are going to interview Graham Balfour. Your team can go through the old files from the Thompson murder. Bring Weaver up to speed when he gets back from his retirement interview. Any questions?'

Nobody had.

'Good. We'll use the incident room for liaising. Get to it people, and I want a daily report. But I'd like DI Miller and DCI McNeil to stay back please.'

They all stood up and filed out. Miller and Harry stayed.

'Right; before you both go off anywhere, Chief Inspector, I want you to go and meet a counterpart of yours from Northumbria police. Detective Inspector Charlie Meekle. He'll be off the Newcastle to Edinburgh train,' she looked at her watch, 'in an hour. Waverley of course. Take DI Miller with you.'

'Why's he coming here?' Harry asked.

'We asked him to come up here and give us some input. He was on the original case, twenty years ago. Tell him that he answers to you while he's up here. Do I make myself clear?'

'Very.'

'Right. Off you go.'

They were dismissed from the room like little boys and outside in the corridor, Harry took Miller aside.

'I just wanted a quick word, Frank.'

'No problem, sir.'

'Sir? Christ, I've been a DCI five minutes. Don't

bother about that stuff unless it's in front of the others. You and I go way back.'

'It's good to see you back on regular duty. Keeps you out of mischief,' Miller said, smiling.

'I can only hope.' He turned around to see his DS standing further along the corridor, looking at her phone.

'How's your new team?' Miller asked, looking at the young woman.

'They seem a decent bunch, to be honest. Stan Weaver ran a good team, but retirement beckoned. He's away in a couple of weeks or so.'

'You're one of the lucky ones, Harry. Some of the others from Standards go downhill. Or else spend the rest of their careers as loners.'

'Norrie nae mates. I had few as it was, but they always had an excuse when I asked them to go for a pint, after I joined Standards. Except you. My landlord.'

'Is that what you wanted to talk to me about? The flat?'

Harry hesitated for a moment. 'Vanessa wants me to have a word with you about giving it up.'

'And you're hesitant.'

'I am. I don't know why. I spend most of my time in her house, but it's just that having the flat is... my sanctuary.'

'It's all the same to me, Harry. If you want to give it up, that's fine. If not, that's good too. But I can see why you're hesitant.'

'You can? Mind enlightening me?'

'You would be moving into a house that is Vanessa's. Yes, it would be your home, but not your *house*. That's the difference. In the back of your mind, you're not sure about taking the leap, in case for some reason, it goes sour. And if it did, you would have nowhere to go. Nowhere to run to.'

'Jesus, you're wise beyond your years, Frank.' He smiled and clapped Miller on the arm. 'How about a pint? Tonight?' He knew he was supposed to be having a beer with Stan, but that wouldn't be a couple, it would turn into another full-blown sesh. Time to give Stan a call and take a rain check.

'Sure. Somewhere that other coppers don't drink?'

'I'll give you a call.'

'Do that, Harry.'

'And if Vanessa sees you and asks—'

'You talked to me about the flat.'

'Good man. Now let's go and pick up that DI.'

'I'm just going to grab my coat. I'll catch up.'

Miller walked away and Harry headed over to where Alex was standing.

'We go way back,' he said to her.

'None of my business.' She looked around. Nobody there. 'But do I get invited along for a pint?'

'No, you bloody well don't. What if I was seen out drinking with another woman? Are you trying to get me divorced? Again? Before I'm even married to her.'

'I never got you divorced the first time.'

'You're going to be a delight! I just know it.'

Alex smiled at him. 'And they said you were going to be grumpy.'

'Who did?'

'Nobody.'

SEVEN

They drove down to the railway station, Miller behind the wheel. There were no cars allowed in the station, which never failed to amaze Miller. They were allowed through because they were police, and they parked the car with a police sign on display.

They stood on the platform waiting for the train to come in, which obliged ten minutes later. It was the King's Cross to Aberdeen, and people started to get off in droves.

'He's here now,' Harry said as they looked along the platform.

'How can you tell?' Miller asked.

'He's the big, tall guy carrying a tartan suitcase.'

'Maybe it's just somebody who's patriotic.'

'Or somebody wanting to impress the heathens,'

Harry said as the man stopped before them and put his case down.

Meekle looked to be in his fifties, with a rough beard that had long ago started to turn grey.

'You two must either be train spotters or you're waiting for me.'

'Charlie Meekle?' Harry said.

'Aye. Or you can call me *Inspector* Meekle if you like.' He spoke in a thick Glaswegian accent, not the Newcastle one they had been expecting.

'I don't like. I'm DCI McNeil. DI Frank Miller. Let's try and not get off on the wrong foot.'

'Aye, nae bother, sir.' He looked at them. 'You might be wondering why I'm not talking in a Geordie accent.'

Miller wanted to get moving. 'My money's on you've been watching *Still Game* on the way up so you can fit in.'

'Good answer, but this time, you'll have to settle for second prize; I'm originally from Glasgow, worked in Edinburgh but transferred down to Newcastle because I felt like it.'

'Right, so now we've cleared that up, let's get a step on. We've a murder to deal with,' Harry said.

'You want to pick up my case?' Meekle said to Miller.

'Not really.'

'What way is that to welcome guests?'

'As the boss said, we have a murder to investigate. If I wanted to carry a suitcase, I'd be working in the Balmoral.'

'Suit yourself.' Meekle picked up the case. 'I'm staying at the Radisson in the High Street. We could drop my case off then go to your station.'

Harry was walking ahead. 'Bring it with you. We'll call you an Uber later on.'

They walked to the car. 'How long since you were here?' Miller asked.

'A long time. Big changes I'm sure.'

Harry got in behind the wheel, saying nothing to the inspector.

'You won't recognise it then,' Miller said.

Meekle was looking out the window of the car like a tourist as they drove down to Warriston cemetery.

'Boy, that was quick. I was just settling in for a road trip,' he said as he got out of the car. 'Will my case be okay in here?'

'I don't think anybody's going to touch your Y's,' Harry said.

'Good point.'

EIGHT

Harry McNeil stood watching the scene unfold before him; Honey Summers was running between some gravestones, hiding behind a large one, before she stepped out and put her hand up towards the man chasing her, and then the man stopped, grabbed his throat and fell to the ground.

'Cut!' the director shouted, and all the crew started moving.

The man on the ground got up, dusted himself down and walked away.

'This brings back memories,' Meekle said.

'I should hope so,' Harry replied. 'That's why you're here, after all.'

Meekle ignored him.

'Good job, Dustin!' the director shouted.

'Who's the pretty boy?' Alex Maxwell asked. She

had driven down with Steffi Walker while Meekle was being picked up at the train station.

'That's Dustin Crowd,' Steffi said. 'You into sci-fi?'

'No. You?'

'Well, I know I'll be watching the first series of the original show before they put the new one out, but I can already tell the second one is going to be my favourite.'

'I got a list of names and told the producer that we'd like to interview everybody who was here on Wednesday,' Steffi said to Harry.

'Okay. Maybe you and DI Miller could start by talking to Honey Summers. I'm going to take Alex to talk with Graham Balfour. Inspector Meekle, keep an eye on things out here.'

A PA showed them into the trailer, which was a bigger, American version of what they called a caravan. This was like a house on wheels.

The actress was waiting for them, still in her costume. She was sitting at a table, smoking, Dustin Crowd sitting opposite.

'They'll be banning smoking in here next,' she said. There was a glass next to her. She picked it up and took a sip from it.

'We'd like to ask you a few questions about last Wednesday, if you don't mind,' Miller said.

Honey shrugged. 'It's fine. It wasn't me.'

'It wasn't you what?' Steffi said.

'Who murdered her.' She gave Steffi a look that stopped just short of *obviously*.

'What did you think of my performance?' Dustin Crowd said to the detectives after they were introduced to him.

'You'll excuse me if I don't ask you to sign my tie,' Miller said. 'We're here to talk about the girl who was murdered last week. Trisha Cornwall.'

'Oh, her. She used to hang about here.'

'You know her, then?'

'Oh yes. There are fans, then there are nutter fans like her. I made the mistake of answering one of her questions on Facebook and she turned from a fan into a stalker. Same with Randy. He did the same and boom – next she wants me to be her baby daddy. And with some crew members, too. She wouldn't leave us alone. I rue the day I answered an email from Trisha Cornwall.'

'Did you ever sleep with her?' Steffi asked.

'That's a bit personal, isn't it?'

'So is murdering somebody,' Miller said. He couldn't fathom why women would fall at this man's feet, although he was starting to imagine the man falling at his feet after he'd clocked him one in the pub.

'I didn't murder her,' Dustin said.

47

'Sorry if we don't take your word for that,' Steffi said, 'so you might have to convince us otherwise.'

'I don't have to convince you of anything. I'm innocent. End of. This is not a trial.'

'How about a trial by public opinion? What happens to your career when people think there's a possibility that you're a killer? You'll light up the Internet with that one. And even if you're not, and we get the real guy, mud sticks. Your name will forever be out there, and this murder will hang around you like a bad smell.'

'Alright. I met her last week. She wanted a signed shirt. That was Tuesday. She told me if I didn't want to sign the shirt, she could always post things on Facebook about me, and I'm talking about personal texts.'

'You could have gotten a lawyer onto her,' Miller said.

'Trust me, I just wanted her to go away. I met her and gave her a signed shirt.'

'And then she did go away, permanently?'

'I did not kill her. I have an alibi, which I will happily provide.'

'Where were you, late Tuesday into Wednesday?' Steffi asked, looking at them both.

Dustin looked at Honey. 'Go on, tell them.'

Honey made a face at him like she'd just stood in something. 'Schmoozing with some of the investors.

We were at a function, all of us. Dustin, Carruthers – he's one of the investors – a whole lot of other people. We were there until late. Then we went back to the hotel. My PA drove me and one of the writers back.' She looked at Miller. 'We had drinks in the hotel bar before I went up to my room. Alone. Dustin went to his, then we spent the night together. We've been an item for a little while now.'

Miller nodded. Her story sounded plausible, but she was an actress at the end of the day. 'Surely people in the hotel would see you going into the one room?'

'We have two adjoining rooms. People *think* we're in two rooms.'

Dustin was grinning. 'Honey and I will be making an official announcement later, and that will only add to the frenzy about the show.'

'When you've been filming scenes in the cemetery, have you noticed anybody strange hanging about? Watching you?' Steffi asked.

'Take your pick. Usually they're lonely old men, looking for an autograph, hoping to be invited in here for a quickie.'

'And that's just me,' Dustin said, laughing.

'Give over,' Honey said, not amused by his joviality.

'Were you here on Tuesday during the day?' Miller asked Honey.

'No, we were filming around the old town. Down by Holyrood.'

'What about you, Mr Crowd?' Steffi asked.

'Listen to you; Mr Crowd! Call me Justin. We're all friends here.'

Miller looked at his notebook. 'How many producers does this show have?'

'Five, I think, but they're not all here. Carruthers Wellington stays here, so he can report back to the other investors. The director is here today, Randy Kline. You might want to give him the third degree. Randy by name, randy by nature. And the second unit director, Mike Peebles.'

'My colleagues are talking to them now. But, do you have many fans here, asking for autographs and such stuff?'

'All the time. They're always creeping about, but it's to be expected. Oh, don't get me wrong; without fans, we don't have a job. But some of them go one step too far,' Honey said.

'Like?' Steffi said.

'Like thinking they can take you out to dinner or home to meet their mother. Some want an auto-graphed pair of panties. Preferably with me still wearing them. Most of them are fine, but some of them are creepy.'

'Well, if you do see something strange, or you

remember anything, please call me.' Miller handed them a business card as he and Steffi stood up to leave.

'You too, Dustin.'

'I will indeed, my good man.'

Outside, some of the crew were wandering about.

'What did you think of her?' Miller said. It was getting warmer now, a hint of what the summer might bring. A few clouds scudded about, as if deciding whether to change direction and come over to piss on them or not.

'Calls herself talented,' Steffi said. 'What talent does she have? She can memorise lines, written by somebody else, be told where to move and how to say those lines by somebody else. Big deal. Another over-paid moron who should look for another job.'

Steffi's breath was coming in gasps now.

Miller looked at her. 'Steffi needs to find a cup of tea.'

'No, I don't,' Steffi said, making a face.

'I could do with one. There's a catering van along the way. I'm sure they could spare us a tea.'

Steffi let herself be led away. Miller knew something was wrong and hoped his DS would talk to him about it.

He looked around him, not wanting to turn his back on any of the film crew or actors; since any one of them could be the killer they were looking for.

NINE

'Graham Balfour?' Harry McNeil said to the face peering at them through the crack at the door. He was holding up his warrant card for the man to see.

'Who's asking?'

'I am. DCI McNeil.'

'What do you want?' His voice rose, echoing off the concrete steps in the hallway. They were on the top floor of the two-storey building. Four doors in the detached block.

'We just want a word. Or would you prefer we stand and talk here? And if you shut the door on me, I will make sure I can come up with some excuse about why I need to enter your house with a warrant.'

'Fine,' Balfour said, stepping back and opening the door wide.

Harry and Alex stepped into the lobby and Harry

turned to watch the man shut the door. *Never turn your back on them if you can help it.* And that was when he was only investigating dodgy policemen.

'You'll excuse me if I don't offer you a cup of tea,' Balfour said, leading them through a door on the right. The living room.

'That's fine. I don't usually drink a lot of tea on duty. I never know when I'll need the bathroom.'

'Och, here we go. That was a long time ago. I'd been out drinking, and I had to go. I mean, there's hardly an abundance of toilets in Edinburgh and the ones that are open stink like nothing on earth. I got caught out. And a patrol car was passing. You know the rest, obviously.'

'We want to ask you a few questions about an incident in the cemetery last Wednesday,' Alex said.

'Okay. Sit down if you like.'

Harry didn't like, preferring to stand. He'd be able to reach his extendable baton faster if he stood. He regularly practised drawing it out in the bathroom. *No pointing in having a baton if it gets caught in a hole in your pocket, Harry, my old son,* Stan Weaver had said to him one day. *There's nothing more dangerous than a dirty cop.*

Alex sat down while Balfour sat opposite, on the settee.

Harry looked out of the front window for a

moment. This detached block of flats had been built at a right angle to the houses next to it. Like it had been an afterthought to the builder, back in the thirties. It seemed like the block had been stuck into St Mark's park itself.

Harry watched as a young mother supervised her child in the playground opposite. Beyond that, trees bordered fenced-in football fields. Further over on the left was a gate that led into allotments.

He turned to face Balfour. 'Where were you on Tuesday night, Graham? You don't mind if I call you Graham, do you?'

Balfour shrugged. 'What do you mean, where was I?'

Harry held out his hands. 'Seems a pretty straight-forward question to me. I mean, were you at work?'

'I don't work. I was with some friends.'

Harry already knew the man didn't work but had wanted to hear how Balfour would answer. 'What do you do with your time?'

'Not that it's any of your business, but I go job hunting during the week.'

'Were you in the cemetery on Tuesday?' Harry asked.

'Yes, I was.'

'Doing what? Job hunting?'

'Trying to get Honey's autograph. On a piece of

paper, not on her panties. You know some guys actually ask for that? I mean, Christ, I can't even imagine.'

'Not your thing?' Harry said, still staring at the man.

'No, it isn't. But Honey's autograph on the cover of a DVD I have of her latest movie is. I can sell it on eBay.'

'Did you see anybody else there?'

'The dead woman, you mean?'

'Yes, that's who we mean,' Alex said.

'Yes, I saw Trisha. She hangs out with us. Or did. There's a group of us.'

'Did you see anybody suspicious hanging about? Harry said.

'Weird, you mean? Half the people watching that show being filmed are weird. But my group and I, we're always respectful.'

'Group?' Harry said.

'My friends. We go all over the UK autograph hunting. It's how we make money.'

'You can't make a living at that, surely?' Alex said.

'Not just autographs. Memorabilia. Get them to sign something and the value shoots up. Especially among those sci-fi geeks. Like, if I got Honey or Dustin to sign a T-shirt, I could make a good few quid off it.'

'They must get bored with you asking?'

'Trust me, they can't tell one face from another. They'll sign anything just to get us to go away.'

'I want to ask you a few questions about Jill Thompson,' Harry suddenly said, seeing if he could throw Balfour off kilter.

'Jill? That was a long time ago.' Balfour stared at the wall for a second, as if picturing Jill Thompson's face there.

'You know why we're asking, don't you?' Alex said.

'Of course I do; she died the same way as the woman last Wednesday.'

'Don't you think that's strange?' Harry said. 'Same thing, twenty years apart?'

'Why would I think it strange? People go into the cemetery all the time, for one thing or another. Never anything good after dark.'

'Do you go there after dark?'

Balfour gave him a look that suggested he thought Harry was winding him up. 'Junkies. They're the ones who go in there. Not like when I was a kid. We used to play in there. Football. We'd take sticks and batter at the giant hogweed that used to grow there. Climb up the ivy to the top of the walls. Play hide and seek. We had fun. Then those older folks discovered it and turned it into a pit. But what did you lot do? Nothing.'

'You were close to Jill, then?' Alex said, ignoring Balfour's barbed comment.

'Not well enough to get her pregnant. Sometimes we hung out. I told the detectives all this back then.'

'I know,' Harry said. 'I read the report. Fourteen-year-old you told the investigators you and Jill would play in each other's houses.'

'Hardly playing, Inspector. We would listen to records. And it wasn't just the two of us; several of us were always there.'

'Did she tell you she was pregnant?'

'No. I read it in the papers.' Balfour held up his hands. 'It wasn't me. I first went with a woman when I was sixteen. A married woman would have some of us guys round and let us have at it. Her husband was a truck driver or something.'

'Did Jill ever tell you if she was sleeping with somebody?' Alex said.

Balfour looked between the two detectives. 'No. A friend of hers did. But she swore me to secrecy.'

'What was his name?'

'She didn't tell me his name. Just that he was older and married but he was going to split up with his wife. He had to be careful, because his wife was jealous and he already had a kid, but he was going to leave her, then he and Jill could move in together.'

'Move in together?' Harry said. 'She was fifteen, man! How could she move in with a man? Technically, he was a rapist. At the very least, he was taking advantage of a young girl.'

Balfour sat back further on the settee. 'I'm just telling you what she told me. I agree with you. And we were all shocked when she died.'

'What about some of the girls she was friends with? You ever talk to any of them?'

'There was Alice. Her best friend. They were thick as thieves. Then when Jill died, Alice wasn't around anymore. I think she moved shortly after.'

Harry remembered the name from the file.

'Do you know if Jill ever talked about her family? Anybody she had a problem with?'

'Are you kidding? Jill was little miss goody two shoes. Or she wanted everybody to think of her that way. Her mother was very strict. If Jill was five minutes late for dinner, her mother would go ballistic. I think maybe Jill rebelled because of it.'

'Are you planning on going back to the cemetery?' Alex asked.

'Of course we are. As I said, it's how I make a living. Plus, you never know, Honey might accept my invitation to dinner.' He grinned at Harry.

There's more chance of her accepting a dinner invitation from the Yorkshire Ripper.

Outside, Harry looked over to the park, as if imagining fifteen-year-old Jill playing with her friends. Like a fifteen-year-old girl *should* be doing.

Not getting ready to move in with a married man.

They went back to the cemetery just in time to see Charlie Meekle get into an altercation.

TEN

Randy Kline blew cigar smoke around the living room area of the trailer. An older man was already sitting down. 'That's all we need,' Kline said, pacing back and forth, 'a dead body near the set. Was it foul play?'

'Yes. She was murdered,' Miller said.

'We need publicity of course, but not the wrong kind. This is history repeating itself.' He stopped to stub the cigar out in an ashtray that was already over-flowing.

'It'll soon go away,' Steffi said.

'Will it? I don't think so. Type *God Complex* into a search engine and you'll see the details about the first murder. It follows the first show like a bad smell.'

'We need to know if you saw anything strange going on last Tuesday into Wednesday.'

'Sit down, please.' Kline waved his hands in the

direction of some seats and sat down near the two detectives. 'You know we're filming a sci-fi show here, with all sorts of strange people going about in costume? Nobody strange would stand out.'

'You allow members of the public to observe,' Miller said.

'We do, but we have stewards keeping them at bay. Most of them just want to watch, but some of them want more.'

'Any of the actors or crew complain about anybody?'

'No. But you could ask him,' he said, nodding to the small man who had just come in.

'What's up?' Mike Peebles said.

'They're questioning everybody about the woman who was murdered last Wednesday.'

'That's certainly going to put this show on the map,' Peebles said.

'You do know a woman is dead, right?' Miller said, standing up.

'Of course I do. But we were just talking about that last week,' he said, nodding to Kline. 'We were thinking of ways to get better publicity for the show.'

'And what better way than to shove a gravestone on top of a woman?' Kline said. 'Except we didn't do anything like that. We were talking about getting stars to tell us how big a fan they were of the original show so we could do a YouTube video.' He looked at Peebles. 'And if you stop talking like a dick, the police might not take us in for questioning or give us a going over.'

'Oh, stop getting your Jockeys in a knot. It's free coverage in the paper.' Peebles walked into the kitchen area and opened the fridge. Took out a bottle of coke. 'I bet her highness is frothing at the mouth.'

'Honey is upset, yes, if that's what you mean.'

'Where were you on Tuesday night?' Steffi said. 'Save us having to come back here with an Alsatian so it can grab your nuts. Just before we give you a going over, of course.'

Miller threw Steffi a look.

'If you must know, we were filming a scene up in Perthshire. Some outside scenes at a castle.'

'He was,' Kline confirmed. 'They were up there with some of the actors.'

'We stayed in a manky wee hotel that served black pudding you could play hockey with.'

'You were all together from Tuesday night until now?' Miller said.

'No. Despite rumours in the *Daily Pish Spouter*, we actually have time off between filming. The crew and actors finished Tuesday evening, and they're not due to be filming again until tomorrow up the High Street. So, they can do whatever they like. As long as their arses are back where they're supposed to be, we don't chain them up in a dungeon.'

The door suddenly burst open.

'I found this guy sniffing about outside.' Meekle pushed the man into the main area of the trailer. Harry McNeil was with him.

'Shovin,' the man said to Meekle, turning round as if he was going to have a go.

'Welly, I think you're sniffing around the wrong trailer. Honey's is further down,' Kline said, grinning.

'What are you doing here?' Miller said, recognising the man.

'Relax, Inspector. It's our very own Carruthers Wellington. Our man in the middle.' Kline turned to Meekle. 'He's our liaison with one of our big investors.'

'Why were you creeping about outside?' Peebles said. 'Nebbin at our conversation.'

'For your information, I was not *nebbin*. I was waiting.'

'What do you need, Welly?' Kline said.

'Look, if this police activity is going to affect the show, I need to know about it. The investors will not be happy if they find out there's somebody been murdered and somebody here is in the frame for it.'

'You can tell them that investigating this murder is more important than your filming schedule,' Miller said.

'Easy for you to say,' Wellington said. 'I have people I have to report to.'

'Let's just deal with it then move on,' Kline said.

'If any of you think of anything, please let us know.'

'What do you make of that Carruthers Wellington?' Harry said.

'I know him,' Miller said. 'He's obviously using a fake name. He's Adrian Jackson's nephew, Brian. Nothing to worry about.'

Harry took Miller's word for it, but thought he might run the man's name through the system anyway.

'I feel like a spare prick at a wedding,' Meekle said to Weaver as they stood in line to get a coffee at the catering trailer.

'Well, I'm here now, and thank Christ they had the good sense to ask you up here for your opinion. I'm sorry I wasn't at the station to pick you up, but I had to talk to somebody in HR about my impending retirement. Waste of bloody time.'

'Don't worry about it. We've got our ears to the ground.'

'What can I help you with?' the caterer said.

'We'd like two coffees,' Weaver said. 'We're detectives. Mind if we ask you a question?'

'Naw, fire away. You want a couple of bacon rolls? Pizza? The production company pays for all of this.' He smiled at them.

'Go on then,' Meekle said. 'Bacon roll, ta.'

'And you, sir?'

'Same. Easy on the ketchup.'

'The condiments are right there, sir.' He turned to a female assistant. 'Two bacon rolls.'

'Coming right up,' she answered.

'What's your name, pal?' Meekle said.

'Tom Robinson. Owner and operator of Robinson catering.' He smiled and swept his hand around. He went to the large urn and poured two coffees.

Weaver looked around to see if anybody was listening, but they were the sole customers. 'Do you get any of the show's fans coming to you for food?'

'Aye, some of them try it, but they get nowt. Food only for the production crew and actors. Some of them cheeky sods try and tell me that they work here but if they don't have a badge, they don't get served.'

'Any of them stand out?'

'One lassie. Well, when I say lassie, I mean, she's no spring chicken but dresses like she thinks she is. Always hanging about with a daft laddie, but again, he's no' a laddie. Looks like he's in his thirties but always wearing one of those graphic tees. They're always here, looking for signatures.'

'You wouldn't happen to know this guy's name, would you?'

'Graham. I heard the lassie call him that. Right pain he is. He's always hovering around here, trying to get free scran. I told him to piss off, and then one day, I saw him getting into a real fight with the woman who was murdered.'

'Do you know what they were arguing about?' Weaver asked.

'Not sure. I was busy. I thought I heard the woman say something about somebody being pregnant. I thought he had maybe got her up the stick or something.'

'Thanks.' The detectives walked away, well out of earshot.

'I told you,' Weaver said, then bit into the roll. Meekle said nothing.

ELEVEN

Aileen Rogers sat and had another glass of wine. Looked at her phone again, at the text message that was there. It made her smile.

Looking forward to seeing you tonight.

She read it over and over and each time she looked at the words, they sent a shiver through her. She couldn't call him, just like he couldn't call her. Spouses on both sides stood in the way. It didn't matter. Chatting online had been the beginning of a journey that was going to end in them both leaving their partners. Texting him – sometimes *sexting him* – was the middle step.

He had asked her if she had told anybody, and she promised him that she hadn't, but he didn't understand how women worked. She'd told her best friend. That wasn't telling somebody, in woman-speak. That was just nature.

He told her that if he got caught, his wife would hurt them both. But once he was away from her, they could start a new life. She couldn't wait.

She closed the text and called her friend. 'Janice. He texted me he wants to meet tonight. I am so excited.'

'Well, you go, girl. You deserve to be happy after all you've been through with that twat.'

'It's been on the cards for years. I warned him a long time ago. But would he listen? No. So fuck him.'

'Nobody will blame you, Aileen. Least of all me. But please be careful when you go with him.'

'What do you mean?' Aileen said.

'I don't mean anything. I'm just saying be careful. You haven't actually met him, have you?'

'That doesn't mean anything. We've talked for hours. I feel like I've known him for years.'

'Not exactly talked though, is it? I mean, chatting on the web and texting isn't actually talking. You could have been talking to one of those robocall things and you wouldn't know it.'

'Jesus, Janice, tell me what you really think. And I don't think that's how robocalls work. Besides, we have spoken on the phone.'

'When?' Janice exclaimed. 'You never told me

that.'

'When he was able to. When his wife wasn't around. I spoke to him last week and he sounds even better than I imagined.' Aileen felt a mixture of elation and anger.

'Still. You can never be too careful.'

'Anyway, Drew will be in any minute, so I have to go.'

'Do you want me to come along with you tonight? I could sit in a corner and just watch.'

'No, that's fine, Janice. I'll be okay.'

'Well, if you're su—'

Aileen cut her off mid-sentence and threw her phone down onto the couch. What a cheeky bitch! Do I want her to come along and sit in the corner of the pub? No, I do not want you to come along and get your fucking cheapies when I'm out with my new man. That was Janice bumped from now on. There was no way she was ever going to tell that slag anything again. Janice was one to talk; she'd gone outside with one of the blokes they worked with at the Christmas night out and dropped her scants for him.

Aileen thought she might just be dropping her own scants for her boyfriend tonight. There was only the slightest bit of doubt creeping about in her mind. His name. He had told her to call him *Buddy* when she had asked him. Oh yeah? What the fuck was that short for?

Buddington? Or maybe it was what his wanker pals called him in the pub when he arrived and they were all pleased to see him. *Budster!* they might shout, clapping him on the back and wanting to buy him a beer as if he'd just crawled through a raging inferno and rescued two puppies. Or successfully shagged some bint he'd met online.

Aileen shook her head. Janice was getting in her brain again. Debbie fucking downer. She didn't know why she hung out with her anyway. Trust, just like in a marriage, was everything in a friendship. She could trust Janice not to say anything to Drew, but after tonight it wouldn't matter.

She heard a car door closing outside their house. That would be Drew coming home now.

He came in, loosened his tie, and put his briefcase on a chair.

'What's for dinner?' he said.

'Whatever you want to take out of the freezer and put in the microwave,' she said, getting up and taking the wine glass and phone with her upstairs.

'Fucking bitch,' he said.

Oh, you don't know the half of it, she thought, ignoring him.

She went into their bedroom and locked the door. She was going to get ready for the love of her life and Drew wasn't going to ruin it.

TWELVE

Harry McNeil was sitting having a beer in the *St Bernard's* bar in Stockbridge when Frank Miller walked in. There were spots of rain on his jacket.

'Jesus, just when I thought it was the start of a warm spell,' Miller said, standing over Harry's table. 'Same again?' He pointed to the half empty pint glass.

'I'll get them,' Harry said, but Miller waved him away and got two lagers before sitting down opposite his friend.

'Cheers, Frank. It's not true what they say about you.'

'It is, Harry.' He laughed. 'Just don't tell Kim.'

'Your secret is safe with me.'

Miller drank some lager before putting the glass on the table. 'I had a call from Percy Purcell before I left the house. They found the next of kin for Trisha Cornwall. She's from down south. The Met have contacted her family.'

'I wonder what she was doing up here?' Harry said.

'She lives up here, apparently. Just moved here a few weeks ago.'

'They have an address for her?'

'They said she was staying with a friend in Leith. Uniform have been there, and the friend says she moved in with a man she met online. Trish was going to give the friend an address, but she hadn't so far.'

Harry drank some more of his pint. 'You'll want to talk to this woman tomorrow. See if she can remember more when she's not quite as upset.'

'I'm thinking it was maybe Graham Balfour, over by the cemetery. How did you get on with him when you spoke to him earlier, sir?'

'Knock that *sir* pish off, Frank. Jesus, I've known you long enough. And Carol, remember?'

'Sorry. Old habits and all that.'

'Anyway, we spoke to him. He's a bit of a wido as well as a weirdo. He and his cronies make their living from getting autographs and the like. He was hanging about the cemetery with the other members of the anorak brigade. And he told us he knew Trisha and she would hang out with him and his mates.'

'It puts him at the scene, if nothing else.'

Harry drank some more then looked at the door, as if expecting it to open.

'You told me Vanessa is giving you a hard time about the flat,' Miller said.

'She wants me to give it up, as I said. To be honest, I'm not ready. Simple as that.'

'Have you tried talking to her?'

Harry shook his head. 'No. I'm always putting it off. I was even going to say I had signed a lease and it was for a year, but she might see through that.'

'Building the foundation of your relationship with a lie. It can only crumble, Harry.'

'Jesus. I can only hope my son grows into a man like you. Little sod will probably end up inside, knowing my luck.'

'But tread carefully, my friend. You don't want to throw away a good thing on insecurities. I'm not telling you how to live your life but, go into this with your eyes wide open. What if you decided not to give the flat up, you split up and then missed Vanessa so much, but by the time you realise this, she's moved on?'

'Christ, listening to you is like eating cheese before bed.'

'Just giving it to you straight. Just don't go home pished tonight and try and talk to her about it.'

'First of all, she's got parents' night at her school, and I'm going to stay at the flat.' He drank some lager.

'Just saying I'm going back there feels good inside. I know that sounds horrible, but your flat is my home. I'm comfortable going there.'

'I get a feeling Vanessa isn't.'

The door opened and in walked a familiar face. Miller couldn't place her at first; mid-twenties, black jeans, wearing a light raincoat.

'Christ, it's Alex,' Harry said.

Miller snapped his fingers. 'Alex Maxwell, your DS.' He should have paid more attention to her in the meeting earlier that day.

'Jesus, don't go shouting it.' Harry tried to disguise his face with his pint glass, but Alex looked over. She was unsure whether to join them so she went to the bar and ordered a drink. G and T, Miller guessed.

After getting a drink she approached their table. 'Hello, sir. Didn't see you there.'

'Yes, you did. You just didn't want to buy us a drink,' Miller said, smiling.

'Nothing gets past you.'

'Grab a seat if you like. It's Harry's round next and he mentioned doubles and I don't think he was talking about a tennis match.'

Alex grinned and sat down.

'I was just telling Harry we've found Trisha Cornwall's next of kin. She's from the London area but moved up here weeks ago.'

'That's a start. It gives us some focus to move forward with.' She drank some of her gin. Looked at Harry. 'I didn't know this was your local, Harry.'

'It isn't. I was just having a pint with Frank.'

She looked at them. 'I can leave you be.'

'Don't be daft,' Miller said. 'We were just discussing the case, but we won't be meeting like this every night. As much as I'd like to.'

'You married, sir?'

'That's a bit forward, isn't it, sergeant?' Harry said.

'Oh, I was just—'

'He's pulling your leg,' Miller said. 'Yes. And I have two daughters.'

'That's nice.'

'What about you?'

'Still waiting for Mr Right.'

Both men looked at each other. *Mr Right doesn't exist.*

'Jesus, here's Stan Weaver,' Harry said, looking at his watch.

The DCI saw him and walked over to the table. 'Where the hell have you been?' he said. His breath stank of beer and he was swaying about.

'The time just got away from me, Stan.'

'That's one thing I like, McNeil: punctuality.' He was slurring his words and he pointed a finger at them all.

'It's only eight twenty. I would have been up in five minutes.'

'Bollocks.'

'Hello, Stan,' Alex said, smiling at him.

'It's DCI Weaver to you. Little upstart.'

'Surely about to be ex-DCI?' she answered, still smiling.

'Don't get smart with me, Maxwell. I still have two weeks in that department so don't forget it.' His face was starting to get red. Miller and Harry both stood up.

'What? You both want to go boxing with me?' Weaver sputtered, trying to remain upright.

'You're going to get lifted in a minute, Stan,' Miller said. 'You don't want to start off retirement in a holding cell, do you?'

'Who do you think you're talking to, Miller? I worked with your dad. He was a real copper. Not like you bunch of pen-pushers.'

Harry put a hand on his arm. 'Come on, Stan, you've had enough.'

'Take your fucking hand off me. I don't need you to tell me how much I've had to drink.' Weaver pulled his arm away and staggered back out. As the door opened, they could see another man waiting for him. The man looked in and then the door shut quickly. Charlie Meekle.

They sat back down.

'He better not be waiting for me outside, Frank, thinking he's got Meekle for company and they can set about me. I've had my fair share of fighting dirty coppers and that pair of bastards will get it, big time.'

Miller put a hand on his arm. 'Weaver couldn't fight his way out of a wet paper bag right now. I don't think they want to go fighting. If they do, they're both finished.'

'Aye, you're right.'

'Well, don't you boys know how to show a girl a good time? I feel like I was auditioning for a new series of *The Sopranos – UK style*.' Alex smiled and sipped at her G and T.

'Stick around. I'm sure there's going to be more.'

'I do like a bit of cabaret. And something to eat. Either of you boys fancy buying a girl a bag of nuts.'

'You're a cheap date.' McNeil stood up. 'If this was a date. Which it's clearly not. I just meant—'

'Dry roasted, Harry, please,' she said, grinning.

'That was a lot of fluff you told me about Weaver letting you call him *Stan*, wasn't it?'

'Yes, Harry.'

'I bloody well knew it.'

She laughed as Harry made his way to the bar.

THIRTEEN

Peter Hanson pulled into the terminus at Balerno and checked the bus was empty of passengers. It was.

He belched as he rubbed his stomach. Fucking fish supper. They were getting more expensive and the portions smaller. He knew he should hit the gym, but he couldn't be arsed. One week of earlies, alternated by a week of a midday shift or backshift. It was hard to get into a routine. That was his excuse anyway.

He opened the back door of the bus and kicked an empty Coke can off. The damn thing had been rattling about there for hours. Those messy pigs couldn't just take their own shite home, could they? He would ban half of them from coming on.

His old man had been a bus driver too, before he croaked it. He smiled as he remembered some of the stories he'd told him. Back in the day, the coffin dodgers would all be lined up at a bus stop, then a voice from one of the control inspectors would come over the airwaves, telling them it was nine am. This was the time the pensioners could come on and put twenty pence in the hopper to use with their bus pass. Not a minute before nine, nor a minute after five, to let the workers get on. His old man would get to a stop close to nine, and they would be like cattle trying to get on and he would open the door and shout to them it wasn't nine yet. He wouldn't let them on. Instead, he would shut the door and drive off, seconds before the inspector would announce the time over the radio, letting the old folks rage at him.

Hanson didn't think he could do that, but his old man was a right bastard. He had pulled his bus over outside Ocean Terminal one night on the backshift, told one of the passengers he didn't feel well, and promptly had a massive heart attack. He was dead by the time the ambulance crew got there.

Hanson wasn't going to be in the job long enough to drop down at the wheel of a bus. He was going to get himself into Police Scotland and his girlfriend was going to help him. Even if it meant him being a Special Constable first. That was always a way of getting in the back door.

If his girlfriend could do it, then so could he. He sat down on one of the seats and took his mobile phone out and called her number. No answer. He tried the house number. Nothing. Nada. Zip. Fuck all. He wondered if she was getting it from one of the neighbours or something.

Fucking bitch.

She better not be out drinking with her pals again. He'd warned her about that. Drinking during the week with that Julie one. She was a bad influence. Well, he, Hanson, would just have to do something about that.

He heard a knock at the front of the bus. He put his phone away. Fuck sake, there was still another ten minutes before he was due to leave; they couldn't stand outside?

He got up as the knocking started getting louder.

'I'm coming,' Hanson said, imagining himself in a police uniform and taking his baton out to the person who was knocking on the door.

FOURTEEN

Aileen Rogers was standing outside *The Dining Room* restaurant down on Commercial Street when she heard the ding coming from her phone.

'Please don't tell me you've got cold feet,' she said in a whisper. She took the phone out and had a look at the screen.

Do you mind if we change plans slightly? I'd rather eat somewhere else if you don't mind. I'll explain in two minutes. Just round the corner. I'm waiting. Get a taxi and I'll give you the money. It's going to be worth it!

She felt a chill wind rushing along the wide, long street, which used to be filled with distilleries or something. Now it was other businesses, including this new restaurant. Fuck. She'd told Janice they were coming here and now that they weren't on speaking terms. If Janice found out, she would have a good bloody laugh at that. She could imagine her so-called friend now; *Where did he take you? McDonalds?*

Aileen sent off a quick text. *Where will I tell the taxi to go?*

Harvey's. It's just along from Malmaison. Just tell him to drop you off at Malmaison, he might not know Harvey's.

B right thr. xxx

A taxi came along a couple of minutes later. Even though *Malmaison* was just round the corner, he was concerned about her safety and didn't want her to walk. What a gentleman! Drew would have had her walking.

'It's not a big fare, but I'll give you a decent tip,' she told the driver. 'My boyfriend just wants me to be safe.'

'No problem, love. The small trips add up at the end of the day.'

He drove along Commercial Street and turned left onto The Shore and down to the end where the hotel was. She handed him some notes.

'Thanks, love,' the driver said.

She got out as the black cab rattled away. There were some people about but nothing like it would be at the weekend. Then her heart sank. What the hell?

Opposite the hotel was *Harvey's* restaurant. And it was closed.

'Boy, do I feel like an idiot,' she heard a voice say

behind her, then she felt a hand on her shoulder and she gasped and spun round.

A man was standing smiling at her. 'Aileen?'

'Buddy?'

'The one and only. But my name's Theo. I had to be sure you were genuine. No offense. I just got here. The taxi driver didn't know *Harvey's* had closed down.'

He held out his hand for her to shake. She felt his strong hand in hers. His smile showed perfect teeth.

'There are other places.'

'Indeed there are, Aileen. I was thinking about the floating restaurant down there, the *Blue Martini*.'

'Oh, I've heard of that but I've never been.'

'It keeps the riff-raff out. Shall we?' He held out an arm for her to hook hers through and they walked through the cool evening air to one of the boats moored on the Water of Leith.

Two doormen stood at the canopy at the end of the walkway that led up onto the boat.

She wondered briefly if they were going to have any trouble getting on, but Theo was dressed in a suit and looked immaculate with his beard neatly trimmed and his hair combed into a fashionable style.

She saw him smile at the two men. 'Gentlemen, good evening.'

The men were used to sizing up people in a heartbeat and one of them smiled at him. 'Good evening, sir, madam.'

Theo indicated for her to go up first. She smiled and thanked him. Drew would never have done that.

Inside, the bar was cosy. Background music played, but not some of that rubbish they played nowadays. This was just setting the ambience of the place.

Theo led her over to the restaurant entrance and a maître d' smiled and showed them to a table overlooking the river.

They ordered drinks and looked at the menu.

'I can't believe we're meeting like this,' Aileen said.

'It's a good thing, though, yes?'

'Of course.' She reached a hand over and put it on his. 'I've been stuck with a husband who treats me like dirt for a long time. I needed to meet somebody who appreciates me. You know, when I was talking to you online, I felt that I'd known you for years.'

'I feel the same way.'

They ordered food and talked and laughed. Aileen hadn't felt so comfortable in a long time.

'What do you normally do for fun?' Theo asked her.

'Fun? I don't know the meaning of the word. I don't have fun anymore. Not with Drew anyway. I do meet up with a little group once a week. That's about as exciting as my life gets.'

'What sort of group? No, let me guess: *The Circus Clown Appreciation Society*?'

She laughed. 'Is there such a thing?'

'I have no idea. But you haven't said yay or nay.'

'It's a little drama group. We put on plays and the like. Just for fun.'

'Do tell me more!' Theo said. 'This is so exciting.'

'It's just for fun. But there's nothing like the rush you get when you're up on the stage in front of people, complete strangers who are enthralled by our performances.'

'That is indeed an achievement. I wouldn't have the guts to stand up on a stage and give it yahoo. I'd be shaking like a leaf.'

'I'm sure you would be fine under pressure.'

You don't even know the half of it. He smiled at her.

'I'd like to use the ladies if you'll excuse me.'

'I'll be here.' They were sitting at a corner table and the lighting was very atmospheric. Theo took the little vial of powder out and quickly poured it into Aileen's drink.

She came back and they drank and laughed.

The waiter brought Theo a steak, well done, while Aileen had a Chicken Parmesan.

And yet, even by the end of the meal, Aileen still didn't know much about Theo. But she planned to change that. Drew was out with his friends and she thought it would be exciting to take Theo home with her.

He had other ideas.

They walked back round to where he had met her. It was dark now, and colder.

'Can I give you a lift?' he said.

'That would be fabulous,' she replied, but then she stopped. 'I thought you said you came here in a taxi?'

'I have to confess; it was a white lie. I wasn't sure how this would go tonight. I've been out with a few women, but most of them were... a disappointment. Undesirables.' He made a face and smiled, putting up a hand. 'I'm not saying I thought you were like that, but if things didn't go smoothly, I could just get in my car without offering you a lift, as you'd have thought I came here in a taxi.'

'I never thought of that,' she said, her smile slipping. 'I thought we knew each other well enough, although we've only talked online.'

'Please don't be offended, Aileen. I get on with anybody and like to have a good time, but some of those women weren't who they said they were. I'm guilty of trusting somebody right off the bat. You included. But this is just a safety net.' He smiled, stepped closer and took her hands and gently kissed her on the lips.

She looked around to see what car he was driving and saw a white van.

'I have an idea, and please feel free to say no, but would you like to come home to my place and have a drink or two?'

Aileen sucked in a breath and practically hauled the van door off its hinges. 'Would I?' She jumped in the van eagerly.

Theo once had a boyhood friend with a glass eye, and they had all teased him about it, saying it was made of wood. *Wood eye.* Aileen's comment made him think of his friend, now a distant memory, separated by time and life.

'No funny business, I promise,' he said.

'No funny business? I was counting on funny business.' She laughed and started to mumble. 'I'm... such a lightweight when... it comes to drink.'

'Luckily I haven't had too much.'

'Well, let's go then.' He smiled and squirmed inwardly at her banging his van door shut. This wasn't a classic Jag – not a classic anything really – but it was his.

Aileen yacked on as they drove from Leith up Ferry Road, and down Warriston Road.

He stopped outside the side gate of the cemetery. Aileen's eyes were so blurred, she could hardly see. The world was swimming around her. 'Are we there?'

'Yes. There's the gates to my house,' he said, laughing inwardly.

They left the van and walked through the gate. 'Up this way,' Theo said, and Aileen started walking. 'I want you to meet somebody.

'When we were talking online, you said you were very unhappy with your husband.'

'I am. I haven't been happy for a long time.' She was slurring her words now and holding onto him for dear life.

'Then I am the man to solve your problems. I am here to make you happy. You see, sometimes when people are unhappy, they just don't know where to turn.'

'I know.' They were walking side by side, and she turned to smile at him. 'I know I'm going to be in a happier place.'

'Oh, you are. I can guarantee it.'

They were walking along the track and Theo dropped back slightly.

'Don't keep me in suspense,' Aileen said. 'Who am I going to meet?' Her eyes were practically rolling.

'Your maker,' Theo said, and brought the hammer down on the back of her head.

FIFTEEN

'It's good to see you smile,' DS Julie Stott said to Steffi Walker.

'I'll second that,' DS Hazel Carter said. The two detectives raised their glasses to Steffi.

'It's being out with you two drunken reprobates that makes me smile,' Steffi said, grinning. They clinked glasses.

'I've just felt a bit down recently,' she said.

'We're always here to lend an ear,' Hazel said, and then she smiled even more when the door to Logie Baird's opened and in walked Kate Murphy.

'Ladies, let me get a round in,' Kate said, eyeing up their glasses.

'I won't argue with that, Kate,' Hazel replied.

Returning from the bar, Kate sat down with the

drinks. 'Having a drink on a Monday night. Rock 'n' roll lifestyle or what?'

'Andy let you out, then?' Julie said.

'Indeed he did. He says I should get what you Scots lassies call, *blootered*.'

'It doesn't sound the same with a London accent,' Hazel said, laughing.

'Hey, I'm trying!' They all laughed. 'But Andy doesn't complain when I go out without him. He knows which one of us cuts up people for a living.'

'Who's got the kids, Hazel?' Julie asked.

'Bruce and his wife.' She held up a hand. 'I know, he went through the mill, but he's fine now. And his wife is great.'

'And the kids are okay staying over?' Kate said.

'They are. Bruce will make sure they get to school okay in the morning.'

The next couple of hours passed in a flash, and at the same time a woman was stepping into a cemetery, Steffi Walker was stepping into a taxi.

'Logie Green Road,' she told the driver.

It was straight down Broughton Street and round the corner to her flat, which was a little garden flat at the back, accessed by walking through the stairwell and out through the back door.

There were only two flats here, one on either side

of the door. The automatic light came on and she had her key out. She opened the door, knowing she wasn't going to be disturbing Peter as he was on backshift.

She got in and before she had a chance to put the hallway light on, a figure stepped out of the bedroom.

SIXTEEN

'Carruthers Wellington?' Adrian Jackson said, turning back from the living room window in his nephew's flat. It was in one of the new apartment blocks built on the old Royal Infirmary site. It overlooked The Meadows park which sat between there and Marchmont. Loved by muggers everywhere after darkness fell, which it now had.

Brian shrugged. His older live-in girlfriend – Rita Mellon – looked at Jackson and gently shook her head in an *I told him* way.

'Carruthers Wellington?' Jackson said again. 'What kind of fucking name is that?'

'Look, hang fire, okay?' Brian said. 'Sit down and I'll explain.'

'Sit down? Are you sure? Just in case the old gin-swilling bastard falls over? Stop being so fucking antisocial and get me a drink. And none of that watered-down pish you give to everybody else. Get the good stuff out for your uncle before he puts his walking cane round your head.'

Jackson had already taken off his signature bowler hat. He sat down on one of the leather settees and looked across at the woman. 'Rita, please. I rely on you to keep our Brian on the straight and narrow.'

'I told him, Adrian. I said, what kind of a stupid name is that? Investments are supposed to be low-key. But does he listen?'

'Clearly not.' He looked over at Brian who was standing at the drinks' cabinet with his back to the room. 'If you're slipping something into my whisky, you know things won't end well, don't you?'

'Jesus, Adrian, I'm not trying to kill you. The most I do is put laxative in chocolate. But not to you.'

'I'll have somebody put something in you if you ever do that to me.' He reached out, took the glass of whisky and sniffed it.

'You know I love you, Adrian. I would never—'

Jackson held up a hand. 'That's enough of that pish. Just tell me what's happening now.'

'Right, it's too late to change my name, because they know me down there. But it doesn't matter; we're getting a two hundred per cent return on our money, but more importantly, we have fifty per cent royalties on merchandise. I had the accountants go over it and we stand to make a small fortune. Plus, the solicitors have made sure we're the only investors for two sequels.'

Jackson sipped his whisky and smiled. 'That's my boy. I can't believe they didn't make sequels last time round. But we'll make sure they do this time.' He put the glass on the table. 'Let's talk about the elephant in the room.'

Brian looked over at Rita, looked her up and down. 'That's not very nice. And she can hear you.'

'Cheeky sod.' Rita glared at him. 'He's not talking about me!'

'I'm just kidding.' Brian was smiling, although the other two knew he clearly wasn't joking.

'The elephant in the room is this woman who they found murdered in the cemetery where the production is taking place,' Jackson clarified.

'The production crew are worried of course, but there's no talk of stopping,' Brian said, taking some of his own whisky.

'There bloody well better not be any talk of stopping. I've sunk a lot of money into this and production is indeed going on. Remember one thing; I have other business partners and they won't be happy. Robert Molloy especially, although Kerry Hamilton is also a fierce one when she gets going. So, if there is any rest-lessness among the ranks, let's quash it right away.'

'I think we could use it to our advantage,' Rita said. 'Everybody likes a bit of controversy. Or some ghoulish goings-on. The fact that a woman was murdered right where the filming is taking place can be put to our advantage. We can capitalise on it by advertising the fact. Something like, *Filmed where a real-life murder took place.* That could be on the DVD packaging.'

'That's brilliant, Rita!' Jackson said, picking his glass up again. He finished the whisky. 'Let's have lunch tomorrow. We can put our heads together and see what else we can come up with.'

'What about me?'

'Sorry, boy, I don't dine with anybody called Carruthers.' Jackson stood up. 'I'll come round about twelve. Wear something expensive. We're going to be eating somewhere upmarket.'

One of his bodyguards was waiting in the hallway outside the door. Jackson had spent twenty-five years in an American prison and he never took his own safety for granted.

Especially now that there was a murderer running around.

SEVENTEEN

Fight or flight. Steffi Walker hadn't shirked away from a fight at any time in her job as an army combat medic, nor during her police career so far, and she wasn't going to back down from a fight in her own home.

She slapped the hallway light on and was prepared to have a go with the man who had just come out of her bedroom.

'Peter! What are you doing?' she said, relaxing as she saw her boyfriend standing there.

'Where the hell have *you* been?' he said, walking across the hall into the living room.

It was a small flat, with the kitchen off the back of the living room. He headed in there, and poured himself a whisky, but by the looks of him, he'd already made a head start.

'Why are you home so early?' she asked him. 'You weren't supposed to finish your shift until after midnight.'

'So, you went out gallivanting? I thought you'd be in. I called from Balerno terminus and got no answer. I was worried sick. So, I called control and they sent a replacement driver.'

'I told you days ago I was going out with some of my colleagues.'

'I don't remember that. But is it too much to ask you to stay in when I'm working?'

'It is, yes.'

He was quick. She didn't see the back-handed slap coming. His hand connected with the side of her face. Then he pushed her hard sideways, her head hitting the doorjamb of the small kitchen.

She lifted her hand, but he reached out and grabbed her by the hair, banging her head against the doorframe again, harder this time.

'You forget I was in the army too, bitch.'

'Let me go!' she yelled, but the little kitchen was out of focus and she found it hard to think.

'Or else what? What is little Steffi Walker going to do about it?' He jerked her head down further now, and she could feel the blood running from her cut lip.

She couldn't speak.

'I didn't think so. Bitch!' He threw her down onto the floor and kicked her hard in the stomach. She gasped, trying to scream, but the pain was the last thing on her mind; he'd kicked her so hard she couldn't take a breath and she started spluttering, thinking she was going to die.

'I'm going out and I won't be back tonight,' Peter snarled, standing over her and pulling a coat on. 'You think about what you did tonight. You understand?'

She didn't answer him, still struggling to breathe.

'I said, do you understand?' he screamed.

She nodded and he kicked her a few more times, on the legs, on the back, on her arm.

At that moment in time, Steffi was more frightened than she'd ever been abroad, serving with the British army.

She thought she was going to die in the doorway of her little kitchen, the one her dad had helped finish. In that second, she thought about calling him, but then her brain kicked into gear and she remembered he was dead.

She had nobody in the world now, and she was going to die alone. She'd be with her dad soon.

After what seemed an age, she managed to take a breath. There *was* one person she could call.

Slowly she tried to get her mobile phone out of her pocket and she finally managed it. The device was on the floor and dazedly she managed to get the contacts page open.

Steffi hit the dial button, got her finger to the speaker button, just before she passed out.

She didn't hear the voice at the other end calling her name.

EIGHTEEN

Harry McNeil woke up with an uneasy feeling. Nothing he could put his finger on right away, but realised when he had showered and was doing coffee.

He was in his own flat and he'd missed a call from Vanessa.

He had assumed she would know he had come here when he didn't turn up, though of course, no one would have known had he been abducted by aliens on the way home. He'd have been poked and probed by the time anybody realised he was missing.

He poured a coffee and debated whether to wet some cardboard and pour milk on it or eat the bran stuff Vanessa had bought him. There were merits for either one as they both tasted the same, but at least the bran had some raisins in it.

'Vanessa,' he said into the phone, talking to the

voicemail. 'I just came here last night as I'd had a few pints. Call you later.' He hesitated, wondering if he should add *Love you* to the message, but didn't in case somebody else heard it, so he ended the call.

Another uneasy feeling, like he got when he had to go to the dentist after procrastinating and the prospect for saving the tooth was anywhere between *We'll do our best* and *This is going to hurt me more than it's going to hurt you.*

Vanessa was pissed off at him, that was clear. He got up from the little table in the living room and pulled the net curtain aside like an old woman trying to avoid the people selling religion from coming to the door. He could see Vanessa's house across the other side of the bowling green, and her car was gone.

He sat back down and finished the cereal. He was sure she would call later, probably at the most inappropriate time.

He was about to leave when his phone rang. 'Vanessa?' he said, thinking that she was maybe using the office phone as her name didn't come up.

'It's me, Harry.'

'Who is this?'

'Alex. I told you last night I'd pick you up to drive you to work. I'm sitting downstairs.'

'Okay. I'll be right down.' God, that was all he

needed, some young woman coming to his flat. Tongues would no doubt be wagging.

He checked the mirror after brushing his teeth. His tie didn't look like a dog had chewed it first. He nodded approval and made his way outside. It was chillier, but the sun was trying to get out of its pit, while the wind was skelping the arse off some clouds. No doubt it would be snowing by lunchtime. Welcome to May in Edinburgh.

He looked around for Alex, realising he didn't know what kind of car she drove. Then she honked the car horn. She had rolled down the driver's window of a shiny little BMW and was waving to him.

Christ, all I need now is Vanessa to come booting round the corner and see me and I'm toast. He didn't wave back, electing instead to duck slightly and pretend he didn't know her until he slipped into the passenger seat.

'Why don't you get one of those clown car horns? I'm sure some of the neighbours round the corner didn't hear you.'

'Good morning to you too,' DS Alex Maxwell said, all smiley and bouncy, like he was taking her out on her first driving lesson. 'Is that what your girlie CR-V has? A clown car horn?'

'It's my wife's car, sergeant,' he said, buckling up. '*My* car's in the garage.'

'Oh yeah? What do you drive?'

'Never mind what I drive. That's not part of the inspector's exam, which you should be more concerned with,' he said as she drove off. The car had a new-car smell.

'There's not much chance of promotion when you land in the cold case unit.' She turned onto Comely Bank Road.

'I wasn't too pished last night, was I?'

'I have no idea. I finished my drink while you stayed with Frank—'

'DI Miller,' Harry interrupted.

'...and I was in bed by eleven. You, I can't account for.'

'I found Weaver. He was waiting across the road for me, full of apologies, slavering about how he hadn't meant it. I didn't have a drink with him. I told him to go home and sober up.' He turned to look at her as she drove through Stockbridge. 'What was he like to work with? I mean, I know him from going to the pub, and I only briefly worked with him in the past, but what was he like on a day-to-day basis?'

'Stan was okay. He was a stickler for the rules.' She briefly looked at him. 'He liked a drink though.'

'You ever see him drink on duty?'

'No. And would I have dropped him in it if I had? No, I wouldn't. We have to trust one another, Harry, and shopping your boss to Standards doesn't get you a Blue Peter badge.'

'You're too young to remember that show.'

'There's always YouTube. When all else fails, there's always YouTube. And Netflix when your next-door neighbour gives you his password.'

She pulled into the car park at the side of HQ. 'Your girlfriend giving you a hard time? Tell me to mind my own business if you want.'

'Mind your own business.'

'Aw, come on. I'm not a gossip. I just feel that we should get to know each other better.'

'Why? You going to name your first born after me?'

She laughed. 'You already know about me, don't you? You know I turn thirty in a few weeks. You can come to my party. Maybe we should have a joint birthday party. You being the big four oh soon.'

'I'll be celebrating mine by taking Vanessa out for a nice meal.'

'No big party?' she asked as they walked across to the entrance.

'Again, none of your business.'

'If you do have your own party, I'll come along, and I promise I won't spoil it by telling everybody it's nearly my birthday.'

'This is two mornings in a row I've come to work with a headache. I'm begging you to stop talking now.'

She laughed as they walked along the corridor. 'If you put a tenner in the kitty, you can help yourself to a coffee in the incident room.'

'I'll get one from the canteen and see you up there.'

'I take sugar in mine,' she said with a smile.

'I don't care what you take. Go put a tenner in the kitty.' He went into the canteen and tried calling Vanessa again, not wanting to smack of desperation, but the suspense of not knowing if she was pissed off at him or not was killing him. He knew he would come out with some flannel about not wanting to disturb her, and that's why he went home.

He took the coffee upstairs.

DC Simon Gregg had lifted a whiteboard off the floor.

Jesus, here we go again.

'Day two of the workplace Olympics try-out?' he said.

Gregg looked puzzled for a second. 'I'm just moving the whiteboard over here, sir.'

'Right.' Harry took his jacket off and sat at a desk. 'Where's DCI Weaver?'

'He's not here.'

'I can see that, Simon. Anybody know where he is?'

None of them did. 'Great. Willie, why don't you give me a rundown before DS Maxwell and I have to go up the high street.'

Young flipped through some papers on the desk before him. 'We went through the witness statements from back then. They all said Jill talked about having a boyfriend but didn't give a name. They thought she was making it up, even when she told them she was pregnant.'

'And Jill's parents?'

'Divorced. They moved away shortly after their daughter's death.'

'We can talk to them later, if it comes to that,' Alex said.

Harry drank some of his coffee. 'Any results from the DNA that was sent to the lab?'

'Not yet,' came from DI Karen Shiels.

Harry felt his headache start up a boot-thumping dance in his head. He took a packet of painkillers out of his pocket and washed them down with some coffee.

'Out on the lash last night, sir?' Gregg said.

'*Out on the lash* is reserved for young blokes like you. I prefer to have a few sociable beers.'

'You're not that old. What are you? Early forties?'

Harry ran through a gamut of expletives but wanted to keep his blood pressure down for the sake of the headache. The boot thumping had already started and he didn't want to introduce the orchestra.

'Thirty-nine.'

'Oh, right.' Gregg looked at Harry for a moment

like he was waiting for the punchline but when none came, he turned away.

Not even had the decency to pull a fucking beamer, Harry thought, but chucked his empty coffee cup in the nearest bin instead.

'I think it's time we got up to the high street, sir,' Alex said, tapping her watch.

Just like Vanessa would have been tapping her watch last night, no doubt, if he'd actually made it back to her place. *What time do you call this?*

'Right. We'll report back with any findings we have,' he said as Alex led the way out.

'You want me to drive?' she asked him as they crossed the car park through a chill wind.

'Silly question, sergeant. Do I look like I could manoeuvre a pool car through traffic without us having to write an incident report at the end of our shift?'

'That's true.'

They got into a scabby Ford that smelled of fish and chips and sweaty socks. 'God knows what goes on in these cars,' he said, cracking a window.

'Surveillance, I think.'

'They eat from the chippie then do a bit of Morris dancing or something?'

'It's the *or something* that worries me.' Alex drove through Stockbridge up Frederick Street towards George Street.

'Still not spilling on the home situation?' she said with a cheeky grin.

'There's nothing to spill, sergeant, and keep your eyes on the bloody road.'

'I told you all about my ex and how we bought a flat together. Fair's fair, Harry.'

'It's DCI McNeil for you from now on. Giving me that spiel about how Weaver let you all call him Stan. I'm surprised you didn't embellish it by telling me he bought you all a drink on a Friday.'

She made a face like she should have thought of that but said nothing. 'Anyway, I just wanted to say, if you ever want to talk—'

'I don't.'

'Let me finish. I was going to say, if you ever want to talk, you can sod off and bore somebody else with it.'

He looked at her for a moment before she laughed. 'Should have seen your face,' she said, heading over Princes Street and up The Mound.

'No wonder Weaver wanted to retire. I'm sure it was a toss-up between that and an early grave.'

They parked in the car park behind the station and walked in through the back door.

'Do you miss this place?' Alex asked.

'No, not really. I can hardly say it was on a par with a funfair.'

'Or visiting a brothel.'

He shook his head. 'Do me a favour; before you get to work tomorrow, make sure you've taken your meds.'

'That sort of remark could land you in front of HR. Or Professional Standards.'

He was looking at her back and couldn't see her face. Then she turned and smiled at him.

He held up a hand. 'Don't tell me; *Should've seen your face.*'

NINETEEN

Miller woke up feeling that, somehow, he'd gone to bed the night before and somebody had broken his neck in his sleep. He was in a chair. He managed to move his head to one side and saw a figure lying in the bed to the side of him.

Light was shining in from behind the blinds. He didn't know where he was.

He gently moved his head from side to side, easing the stiffness, and then he remembered: Steffi!

He got up and used the bathroom and then went to find a doctor.

A nurse had said there was a room that was used for families who needed to stay overnight and had let him sleep there, promising to come and get him should things change. She had given him a travel toothbrush and a little tube of toothpaste. He just needed a coffee to function. He found one down in the canteen.

'How's she doing, doc?' Miller asked, as he came back onto the ward. He felt chilled inside even though it wasn't cold in the hospital.

'She's bruised and has a slight concussion, which is bad enough, but I was told there was blood on a door-jamb, so we're working on the assumption that her head was hit against that. She was lucky. I've seen worse brain damage from a lesser strike. She's going to hurt for a while, and I want her kept in for a couple of days for observation. But again; she was very lucky. This time.'

'She's going to be alright though, isn't she? Long term, I mean.'

'I'd put money on it, though nobody can ever say a hundred per cent. But yes, I'd say so. She had a severe beating, but nothing is broken and the bruises will heal. I can't speak for the mental scars.'

'Can I go and see her?' Miller said.

'Not too long. She's still in pain.' The doctor walked away.

He walked along to her room and found Steffi sitting up, attached to a drip. There was a bandage round her head and there was a monitor hooked up to her too.

'I thought I looked bad until you came in,' Steffi said, her voice raspy.

'Jesus, Steffi,' Miller said, looking at her.

'Nice to see you, too.' She looked at him. 'No, it really is.' Then she started crying.

'Come here, you big girl,' he said and went over to the bed. He hugged her as best he could before he gently pulled away.

She sniffed and took the paper hanky Miller had handed to her from a box by her bed.

'What happened, Steffi?' he asked her.

'It was something over nothing. It's not a big deal.'

'Of course it is. You called me and if you hadn't, God knows what would have happened.'

'I'm not pressing charges, Frank. I can't.'

He leaned closer. 'Who was it?' He knew but he needed her to tell him.

'It was Peter, of course, but you already knew that. But listen; he was just upset that I was out and didn't hear him calling from the Balerno terminus. He was worried.'

'Has he ever done this before?'

She swallowed like her throat was getting dry and Miller poured her a little glass of water. She tentatively took it and swallowed some. 'Yes,' she said, putting the glass down.

'How often, Steffi?'

'He just has a bit of a temper, that's all. It's the stress of driving the bus all the time. You know, people shouting at him, threatening him. He doesn't mean it.'

'Stress?' Miller said. 'Just like our job?' His muscles tensed with anger.

'He'll be fine when he's on the force with us, I'm sure. He said we knocked him back before, but he's got it all under control now.'

'He wants to be a copper?'

Steffi nodded. 'He's ex-army like me. He'd be good in uniform.'

Miller put a hand on hers. 'You rest. I'll post a couple of officers on your door.'

'There's no need.'

'That was an FYI. It's happening, sergeant.'

When two uniforms appeared, they said their goodbyes and Miller left, speaking to the uniforms on the way. 'You do not, under any circumstances, let her boyfriend near her. He tried to kill her last night.'

Both men stood up straighter, maybe at the prospect of giving Hanson a lobotomy with an extendable baton.

A fucking copper? Miller thought as he made his way along the corridor. Over my dead body.

He knew Steffi was making excuses for him. It was classic domestic violence syndrome. He called his wife at home.

'It's out of her hands now. That went beyond domestic last night. That was assaulting a police officer. Maybe attempted murder, if we can get Norma Banks on board,' he said.

Miller knew his mother-in-law, and Procurator Fiscal, could throw the book at Hanson.

'I'll talk to her, Frank. Just make sure Steffi's safe.'

TWENTY

They were in Kelty, a twenty-minute drive up the
motorway, which would have taken longer, Harry
thought, if Alex hadn't been driving like Stirling Moss.

'This isn't your fancy wee German sports car
you're in,' he'd said, sure his life had flashed before his
eyes a few times on the way up.

'We'd have been here even quicker if it had been,'
she'd replied, smirking.

'If you were my daughter, you'd be bloody well
grounded by now. No pub, no phone, no nothing.'

'I'm a first-class driver.'

'Says who?'

'Says me.'

'Did you read that in your horoscope this
morning?'

Harry stretched his back. Not only did the pool car stink, it had all the comfort of Fred Flintstone's car.

His son also lived in Kelty, a few streets away, and the thought of his boy not living with him anymore made him wish he'd been a better husband.

His phone rang as he stood out on the pavement, looking down at a corner shop near the roundabout, where a few ne'er-do-wells with hoodies on, were eyeing up the car. He prayed they would nick it.

'Harry? It's Frank Miller. We got another shout to go down to Warriston cemetery. We have a second victim.'

'Jesus. Under a grave?' He waited while Miller spoke to somebody, his voice muffled now as if he had put the phone against his jacket.

'No, different this time. I'll explain when you get back. Can you come over here when you're done with that woman?'

'Will do.' He hung up, the wind ruffling his hair. Kelty was a windy town just off the motorway and exposed to the elements.

'Bad news?' Alex asked as Harry knocked on the woman's door and waited for a response. They'd called ahead to make sure she would be in and she'd promised she would.

'What gave it away? Me saying *Under a grave*?'

'Just asking. And if she offers us Tunnock's

Teacakes with a cuppa and there's only one, I'm going to eat it. And I hope there's only rich tea left.'

'Your father obviously spared the rod, but yes, it's bad news. There's another victim in the cemetery. DI Miller wouldn't go into details.'

'I wonder why Frank's keeping things close to his chest?'

'It's *DI Miller* to you. How many bloody times do I have to tell you?'

'Sorry, Harry.'

'Jesus.'

This flat was in a block of four, with the door on the outside, up a short flight of concrete steps.

The woman answered the door and pulled her cardigan closed, as if the chill wind was ever present.

'You're a hard woman to track down,' Harry said.

'I got remarried after... well, you know...'

Harry nodded his head, indicating that he did indeed know.

'Come in,' she said, stepping back.

Harry and Alex stepped over the threshold and immediately went up a short flight of stairs into the flat proper.

'Would you like some tea and biscuits?' she asked.

'Yes, please, that would be great,' Alex said.

'I hope it's all rich tea,' Harry whispered to Alex. 'That would teach you.'

'I hope you like custard creams?' she said a few minutes later, coming in with a tray.

'You shouldn't have gone to the trouble,' Alex said, not meaning it and looking at the plate to see if there was a teacake lurking there that had maybe fallen out of the box; but it was indeed some custard creams.

Harry took the coffee and added milk. 'How long have you been using the name Dignan? If you don't mind me asking.'

'I stopped being Mrs Thompson four years after Jill died. Our marriage didn't survive. It died the day Jill did.' She sipped at her own cup of tea, ignoring the biscuits.

'I'm sorry to dredge up the past,' Harry said as Alex palmed a biscuit like a magician and ate it quietly.

'I figured you would be coming round again, after I saw it on the news about that poor girl.' She looked at them both in turn. 'I'll do anything I can to help you catch whoever did this.'

'Thank you.'

'You don't think it's the same man who killed Jill, do you?'

'All we're working on right now is, the manner of death is similar. We can't rule anything out at this point.' Out the corner of his eye he caught Alex catching some crumbs in her hand. What are you going to do with them? he wondered.

Then she answered his unasked question by swiping them onto the tray.

'We know Jill was pregnant at the time of her death,' Alex said, as if *the big crumb incident* hadn't happened. 'Did you know if she had a regular boyfriend back then?'

'Good God, no!' Mrs Dignan answered, and Alex wondered for a second if she was protesting about the disposal of the crumbs. 'No, she would never have had a boyfriend at that age. I know some girls do, but not Jill.'

Alex softened her voice before carrying on. 'Mrs Dignan, I know this must be hard for you, but Jill was obviously seeing a boy. Did you ever hear any of her friends talking about him?'

Dignan took a deep breath and let it out. 'No. I never really had much doings with her friends. I wasn't the *cool* mum. They all liked to hang out at that other house. The one where anything goes. I hated her going there but it only caused a fight when I protested, so most of the time I said nothing, just to keep the peace.'

'What house was this?' Harry asked.

'The one near the park, on the other side of the walkway. The Balfour house.'

'Graham Balfour's house?'

'The same one. I did not like that boy at all. He was a weirdo.'

Still is, Harry thought but kept it to himself. 'Why would Jill go there?'

'Because of the Balfour girl. She was their leader, the one they all wanted to hang out with. They would go to her house and do God knows what. I smelled smoke on Jill a few times so I think the Balfour girl encouraged them to smoke.'

'Do you think that Graham Balfour could have been the boy she went with?' Alex asked.

'I doubt it. He was one of those boys who was borderline spastic.' She looked at the two detectives, as if saying the word out loud would be cause for them to put her in handcuffs. 'I know we're not supposed to use that word anymore, but it's true. He was. He acted like he was daft. I hated Jill going near him and warned her not to, unless the sister was there.'

'Did he ever touch her, to the best of your knowledge?' Harry asked.

'No, not that I know of. I think she would have told me, but that little besom Balfour would have encouraged Jill to go with a boy, I'm sure.'

'Did she ever mention anything about going to watch the filming in the cemetery?' Alex asked.

'Did she ever! I can't remember who was in that stupid show, some smarmy sod who shoved an old wig down his shirt front to make himself look macho. Made him look like a monkey more like.'

Harry flipped open a notebook, pretending to read from it. He didn't want Mrs Dignan to think he was a fan of the show, which he had been. He'd been in uniform at the time, but he'd been into sci-fi big time.

'Randy Kline?' he said, as if he'd just read his own notes.

'That was it!' Mrs Dignan said, snapping her fingers. 'Randy bloody Kline. What did he go on to do? Nothing. I haven't heard of him again, have you?'

'He went behind the camera. He's actually directing the remake of *God Complex*. So I heard, through the investigation,' he quickly added in case either woman thought he was a member of the Kline fan club.

'I don't know how old he was at the time, but he had to be in his late twenties. Dirty bastard. If her father had thought for one moment that Kline had touched Jill, the only thing he would be directing now is his wheelchair.'

'He was twenty-four, according to the report I read,' Harry said.

'Same diff. He's still a dirty bastard.'

'Do you know if she ever had any direct contact with Kline?'

'I heard the girls whispering in Jill's room one evening, on one of the rare occasions they actually came over. Jill said she wanted to meet Kline soon.'

'Wanted to, or was going to?' Alex prompted.

'I think she was at the stage she just wanted to meet him in person, like she had a schoolgirl crush on him. I don't know if she ever did. But I told the police all this at the time.'

'I'll look for the original report,' Harry said.

'Have you spoken to Trisha Cornwall yet? I don't know if she got married, mind, so she might be going by another name, but they were good friends too.'

Harry looked at Alex before carrying on. 'No. Trisha's dead.'

'Oh, I'm sorry. She might have been able to throw more light on it. I know the police spoke to her at the time, but you know how you remember things much later.'

'I have people looking through the old reports.'

There wasn't much else the woman could tell them, so they left.

Outside, the sun was out but the persistent wind was still there, blowing Alex's blonde hair round her face as Mrs Dignan closed the door softly behind them.

'I can't believe you ate a biscuit,' Harry said as they walked down the short flight of outside stairs.

'Why? I work out. I can burn it off.'

'Are you suggesting for one minute that I can't?'

'Of course you can, Harry.'

'I can.' He shook his head and put his seatbelt on. 'What do you make of this Kline guy?'

'I think you know more about him than you're letting on,' she said, starting the car. It rattled like a bag of spanners as she drove up the road. The car hadn't been touched while they were away; not even the neds had taken a fancy to it.

'I'm a fan of the show. I knew Kline was back directing, that's all. I saw his name in the report, that he'd been questioned but was quickly ruled out.'

'Ruled out by who?'

'Probably his lawyer. Back then, he was a pretty big deal, so his face was everywhere. In mags, on TV. If he was messing around with Jill, he must have been very careful about it.'

'Maybe he invited her into that caravan thingy they hang out in, in between takes.'

'The Americans call them trailers.'

'It's a fancy caravan. My mum and dad used to have one. He loved pissing off the drivers behind him when they used to drive up north.'

'Do they still drive it around?'

'Nah. They fly to Spain nowadays. Let somebody else do the driving.'

'Can't fault that logic. Now, I'm going to let you do the driving, back to Edinburgh, down to Warriston cemetery. Grab something at the drive-through first. Harry's starving.'

'That's not going to be a thing, is it?'

'What?' he said as she got on the slip road for the M90.

'This, talking in the third person stuff.'

'Harry doesn't want to talk about it.'

'You're annoying.'

He grinned at her. 'Harry doesn't seem to think so.'

TWENTY-ONE

The charred body hanging from the tree in the little walled-off section of the cemetery had been photographed and videotaped. The ground beneath the hanging corpse was burnt.

'This is worse than the last time,' DCI Weaver said, coming up behind them. DI Charlie Meekle was by his side, like an ever-present lapdog.

'He stopped at the one killing, twenty years ago,' Harry said.

'I know that.' Weaver glowered at him.

'I wonder why this time round, there's a second victim,' Frank Miller said. He'd seconded one of the other sergeants on his team to help while Steffi Walker was in hospital.

'Well, DI Miller, I know about this as I was the

lead investigator on the case. Twenty years ago. While you were running about in shorts. Did you read up on the last case?'

'I lived through it.'

Weaver looked puzzled. 'What?'

'I lived over there. I was only about ten or so when the girl was murdered here the last time.'

'Were you one of those wee bastards who used to climb up on the wall next to the caretaker's house and shout abuse at us?'

'I don't remember doing that. It was probably some of the older boys.'

'Aye, I'll bet.' Weaver turned his attention back to the woman who was slowly being lowered down. Meekle stood close to him.

DI Maggie Parks walked over to Harry. 'There was a handbag on the ground nearby. The driving licence is for a female, so for now, we'll assume it's her. Aileen Rogers is the name on the licence. The pathologist can confirm or deny later.'

'This is DI Meekle up from Newcastle,' McNeil said, introducing them. 'I don't believe you've been introduced.'

'Good to meet you,' she said, without much enthusiasm.

'It's *sir*,' Meekle said, his tough Glaswegian accent growling out.

'This is DI Maggie Parks, pal. And if I ever hear you talk to her like that again, your arse will be put on a train back down south so fast there will be friction burns on the seat. Do you understand me?'

'I do indeed.' He looked at Maggie. 'My apologies, Inspector. It won't happen again.'

Weaver looked at the DI but didn't say a word.

Miller looked at the charred figure, hanging from the tree by its neck.

'How come the rope isn't burnt?' Meekle said. The sun was out, making the scene seem surreal.

'It's a steel rope,' Maggie Parks said.

'I was asking Miller there, to see if he knew,' Meekle turned to her with a smile. 'But getting you to answer for him is cheating. Just so you know.'

'Just keep your mind on the job, Meekle,' Harry said. 'And I want a full report about the Jill Thompson case from you later.'

'Rest assured, we'll be swapping notes, sir.'

DS Hazel Carter took Miller aside. 'Sir, we ran a check on Peter Hanson; Lothian Buses said he called them up and said he had a family emergency. His uncle was in a car crash last night down in Cumbria so he'd be off for a few days.'

'Let me guess; he doesn't have an uncle in Cumbria?'

'He doesn't have an uncle. Period. I called his ex-wife and she told me. His work also said the address they have on file for him is Steffi's place. His mum and dad are dead, and the house they had was sold years ago.'

'So, where the bloody hell is he?'

'Maybe he's on the run. He must know we're all looking for him,' Hazel said.

'I think he's laying low somewhere so he can get to Steffi. So he can talk to her and persuade her not to press any charges.'

Miller's jaw tightened at the idea.

'You may well be right.'

He turned when they started to lower the corpse. The SOCOs gently laid her on the ground, out of respect.

Maggie Parks crouched near the figure, once a human being, now reduced to a black hulk. She shone a little torch at the head. Then she stood up and addressed Harry.

'I can't say for definite, but she looks to have a round hole in the back of her head. Just like the last one.'

'So, burning her would have just been for show, if she was already dead,' he said.

'Looks like it.'

Alex came across to Harry. 'I had a call from the tech guys. They got into Trisha Cornwall's phone. She sent two texts the evening she died.'

'Do we know who to?'

'The phone company were on the ball; there were a load of texts and calls to one number in particular, before the last texts. That number belongs to Randy Kline, one of the directors.'

'And the other one?'

'Graham Balfour. The guy who was a suspect in the original murder twenty years ago.'

'Sounds good to me. I'd like another crack at him. He's hiding something, I'm sure of it,' Harry said. 'I'll go with Alex and talk to him again.'

'I can come with you,' Miller said

'We'll do it, Miller,' Weaver said. 'You stick to this woman here. Meekle, stay with Miller.'

Meekle nodded and Miller turned to look for Hazel Carter. He saw her and walked over. 'Has anybody found Peter Hanson?'

'Not yet, sir. Not that I've heard.'

'Right. Contact our recruitment department and have them red flag Peter Hanson's name. *Do not employ*. Explain to them why.'

'Will do.'

'We can walk, if you like, sir,' Alex said to Harry. 'It's just over there.' Miller heard her and looked along to the end of the cemetery extension. He remembered climbing up a huge gravestone when he was a boy and it was time to go home for dinner.

'Fine by me. Our car is boggin'. God knows what those surveillance boys get up to in there.'

Weaver looked at Miller like he wanted to rip his head off but strode away after Harry.

TWENTY-TWO

'That was bad patter,' Weaver said to Harry as they left the cemetery and started walking along the pavement. He looked at Alex to see if she was listening, but she was walking ahead.

'What are you talking about, Stan?' Harry said.

'It's *Stan* now, is it? Been a fucking DCI for five minutes and respect goes out the window?'

'Jesus. Give me a break. If you've got a problem, spit it out.'

He stopped so suddenly that Harry thought Weaver was going to smack him.

'Spit it out? Okay, I fucking will. I've given you the benefit of my wisdom when it comes to running the cold case unit. Took time out of my life to have a drink with you and how do you repay me? Go drinking with your new pals instead of meeting me like you said.'

'For God's sake, get a grip of yourself. I was late, that's all. What else have you got to do with yourself? You're a widower. You can have a drink anytime, especially now since you're about to retire. I don't see the big deal.'

'Don't you talk about my Nettie like that! Who the fuck do you think you are, McNeil? Just a jumped-up DI who nobody wants to work with.'

'I want to work with him,' Alex said, coming back towards them.

'Who asked you? You're another loser. You're just a wee hoor that will never make it up the ladder without giving it to McNeil here.'

'That's enough, Weaver. You're going to cross a line here.' McNeil thought he smelt drink on Weaver's breath.

'You'll never come up to my standards, you jumped up little...' Weaver grabbed hold of the front of Harry's suit and drew his fist back. Harry stood his ground.

'Go ahead, Stan.'

'What then? Run back and grass me, you snivelling wee shite. Once a rat, always a rat, eh?'

He pushed Harry away and started to walk away.

'Where are you going now, Stan?'

'Mind your own fucking business. And remember one thing; until I retire, *I'm* in charge of this department.' He turned to Alex. 'I want a full report from you, Maxwell. I want to know everything about Balfour.'

Weaver stormed off, not looking back, going back the way they had come.

Alex's face had gone red. 'Well, he can whistle for it. Talk to me like that. Who does he think he is?'

Harry straightened himself up. 'I think he drinks too much.' He patted her on the arm. 'Come on, let's go. Weaver won't be around much longer.'

It was actually warm now and Harry was sweating by the time they crossed over the footbridge that was adjacent to the old bridge that spanned what was once a railway line and was now the Leith to Broughton cycle lane.

'He might not even be in,' Alex said.

'He is,' Miller said. 'I just saw the curtain twitching on the side window, the one facing us. He must be looking out to see if he can see anything that's going on in the cemetery.'

When they got into the communal stairway, it felt good to be in the shade. Upstairs, the front door was ajar.

'It's open!' Balfour shouted from inside.

Harry led the way in, ready for combat, but none came.

'I made some tea. I saw you coming.'

'We know,' Harry said.

'Jesus, this is exciting,' Balfour said.

'Exciting?' Alex said. 'A woman is dead.'

'Exciting for us, I mean. This is our business.'

'No, it's *our* business,' Harry said.

Balfour indicated for them to sit. The place was quite tidy for a bachelor.

Alex sat on a leather couch, Harry taking a chair, making sure they could still see him in case he suddenly came at them with a sword or something.

'I want to know why you didn't tell us about Trisha Cornwall texting you the night she died,' Harry said.

'I told you I knew her. She was part of the group. I wasn't hiding anything.'

'Sit down, Mr Balfour.'

Balfour sat on a dining chair at the small dining table.

'She was murdered, and you were probably the last person who spoke to her,' Alex said.

'I would think the murderer was, wouldn't you?' he replied.

'Don't be pedantic,' Harry said. 'Why was she texting you before she died?'

'Should I have a lawyer present?'

Harry stood up. 'Listen, Balfour, you are our number one suspect. We can either talk here, or we can take you to the station and keep you there for hours. Your choice.'

Balfour grinned and held up his hands. 'Alright, alright. No need to get tetchy.' He paused as Harry sat back down. 'The thing is, Trisha was unstable. And by that, I mean she would attach herself to somebody and find it hard to let go. She was all-in when she found a new friend. She wanted their friendship to be exclusive. Then she would pester that person. Emails. Texts. She was a real pain in the arse. When you were friends with her, you were *hers*. And if she asked you to start messaging on Facebook, look out. God forbid you speak to somebody else.'

'She was a stalker, in other words?' Alex said.

'Oh yeah. I told her, you're daft doing that. We ask people for autographs, but Trisha took it a step further. Always wanting exclusive friendship. Then she got entangled with Randy Kline. You need to go and ask him. He friended her. I mean, Trisha was nice looking, don't get me wrong, but so is a Rottweiler. As soon as Kline thought he was on to a good thing, she had her hooks into him. She wouldn't leave him alone. I told her she was being stupid, but what do I know?'

'Did she ever talk about meeting Kline in person?'

'Of course! By God, the woman was insatiable when it came to stalking celebrities. Her crowning achievement was when she was served a restraining order. She had been stalking an author and wouldn't leave him alone. I'm surprised she didn't get a hammering before now. She was like a nice delicious-looking cake on the outside, full of maggots on the inside.'

Harry raised his eyebrows at Alex. *Maggots.* 'Did you see her on the night she died?'

'I did. Early evening. We were hanging about in the cemetery. Autograph hunting. But there was a group of us and I was never alone with her. Me and my pals were together then we came back here, without Trisha, I might add.'

'Did you know Aileen Rogers?' Harry asked.

Balfour looked into space for a moment, like he was looking at the calendar on his wall for inspiration. 'Nope. Doesn't ring a bell. Why? What's she done?'

'She's dead.'

'I'm guessing she was either killed in the cemetery or was left there.'

The detectives were silent for a moment. 'Why would you say that?' Harry asked.

'I saw the flames last night. Late. I didn't call the fire brigade or anything. I thought they were filming a scene from the show. You know, the one where the woman gets burned to death? They're following the original script quite closely, and putting their mark on it of course. So, when I looked out and saw the flames, I thought that was pretty good.'

'What time?' Alex asked.

'After ten. Something like that. But let me ask you, that's two deaths like the characters in the script; do you think he could be following the original script? If so, then that's not the end of the deaths.'

Harry didn't answer. He just knew from the original show that four more people died a painful death.

Including the policeman who was investigating the case.

TWENTY-THREE

The man walked slowly through the tall grass, his dark suit a stark contrast to the shades of green. He looked up to the sky, his arms spread wide.

The woman lay on her back, her hands tied behind her. Her clothing hadn't been touched. He looked down at her now, his blazing eyes piercing into hers like pinpoints of sharp light.

He brought his arms down and smiled at her. He could have been a lover come to rescue the damsel, if it weren't for the hammer he was holding in his hand.

A slight wind ruffled his hair. He didn't take his eyes off her as his face got closer to hers. He knelt down, maintaining eye contact.

'It's not going to be long now,' he said. 'I'll make it all go away. I'll take you away from this. You won't ever

have to suffer again. You won't ever have to suffer those fools again.'

She couldn't hear him. She didn't struggle as he put the rope round her neck and started hauling her upright, the rope sliding easily round the branch of the large tree. When she was above the pile of dry branches, he lit it and stood back, watching as the flames crept ever closer to her skin.

'Cut!' Randy Kline shouted. 'Good job, everybody. Dustin, that was amazing as usual.'

Kline turned away as Dustin Crowd helped the actress to her feet.

There was a small crowd of onlookers out of sight of the cameras and a cheer went up when Dustin was finished, and he smiled and bowed in their direction.

Harry was standing with Alex and Miller.

'Where did Weaver go?' Harry asked Miller.

'I thought he was with you?'

'He was, then he flew off the handle and stormed off. If ever somebody needed to retire, it's him. Just as well he's going in a couple of weeks, or he'd be booted out the door.'

'What happened?'

'Just an altercation. I've recommended officers be

fired for less, when I was an investigator. Where's Meekle?'

'I have no idea.'

Honey Summers walked over to them and stopped in front of them. 'Inspector Miller? I just wanted to talk to you in private.'

'This is DCI McNeil. He's in charge of the investigation.'

'We can step out of the way and talk,' Harry said.

'I'm scared, Inspector.'

'Scared of what?' Miller said.

'Somebody here.' She looked around to make sure they weren't being overheard. 'I heard somebody talking. About killing somebody.'

'You need to tell us who this was,' Harry said.

'I'm not sure who it was.'

'Who were they talking to?' Miller said.

'I'm not sure. I didn't hear another voice. Maybe they were talking on the phone?'

'We can have somebody shadow you while you're working here if you feel unsafe.' Harry said.

'That would be good.'

'I can assign one of my female officers.'

'Thank you.' She made to turn away but stopped. 'Somebody said that a woman had been burnt to death in the small extension part?'

'We can't go into details,' Harry replied.

'She was hit by a hammer then he hung her up and set fire to her corpse, with a little bonfire underneath her.'

'Did you see something?' Miller said.

'It's the script,' she said, looking into the distance. 'The girl under the gravestone. The woman being burnt. Both of them had a hammer to the head first, so he could manipulate them. It's how the women in the script die. They're killed by God.'

'God?' Harry said, getting an uneasy feeling.

'Somebody with a God complex. That's where the title of the show came from. I won't give the ending away, but my character's next. The actress who was just being murdered by Dustin Crowd? She's before my character. Then I'm next. He puts a bag over my head to kill me. That's how my character dies.'

Harry looked at her, at the worry lines on her face. Without make-up, she looked normal, and he could see the natural beauty in her. 'Do you know the women who have been murdered? Trisha Cornwall and...' he hesitated, 'I can't say her name before next-of-kin have been informed.'

'Trisha Cornwall was a bitch. But I told Randy, if you sleep with her, you'll never get rid of her. But what do I know? He had his way and then she came back at him like a leech.'

'Do you think he could have killed her?'

'I don't think so. You never truly know somebody though, do you?'

Harry thought about Stan Weaver. 'Anyway, Miss Summers, are you going back to your trailer?'

'Yes. I'm supposed to be getting made-up by my personal make-up artist in the make-up trailer, but she didn't show for work. Aileen's never late for work, so one of the other girls is going to do it. Randy will fire her for sure.'

'Aileen who?' Harry said.

'Rogers. If you see her, get her to get a move on, but I can't see her coming in to work now.'

'Me neither,' Harry said, as Honey Summers walked away. Aileen Rogers would never turn up for work again.

TWENTY-FOUR

Mike Peebles peeked through the curtains in the trailer. 'They'll come looking for you. It's only a matter of time.'

'And then what? Randy Kline said. 'That mental cow was asking for it. Stalking people like that. Didn't she have a boyfriend or something?'

'She did, but obviously his manhood wasn't in the eye-watering category.'

'I bet she didn't tell him she was messing around.'

Peebles stepped back from the window. 'You couldn't help yourself though, could you? I mean, you couldn't keep it zipped up just one time.'

'Christ, what are you now, my dad?'

'Fine. I'm only trying to help. You fairly fucked off after that last scene, but what do I know? And what was Honey doing talking to that copper?'

'I couldn't tell. I was too busy fucking off, according to you.'

'Well, you were, Randy. You know they're going to come and talk to you and they're going to assume you killed that stalker bint, and Aileen.'

Kline looked at him. 'Who's Aileen?'

'The woman who looks like she'd been on a spit. The cooked one.'

'Isn't she the make-up woman?'

'One of them, yes. But I heard some talk. They think it's her.'

'That's the second one killed who's associated with this show. I know Trisha was a nutter but she was connected through me.'

'Now she's dead,' Peebles said.

'Mike, this is going to put us on the map. There's already a buzz on Twitter and Facebook about the show. What with me starring in the first one and directing this one, we're going to go viral.'

'You better hope so, or else Carruthers will go back to whoever is bankrolling this project and tell them we're a couple of con artists.'

'Speak for yourself. And that half-brain should have just stuck to using his own name.'

'You know who's behind this, don't you?' Peebles said.

'I couldn't care less to be honest. I'm making a good wage from this and I'm going on to better things.'

'*We* are going on to better things.'

'Yeah, yeah.'

'However, we need to focus on the here and now, not having our names on the Hollywood walk of fame,' Peebles said.

There was a knock at the door. 'That's either Honey, deciding she should stop fighting her feelings for you, or it's the coppers who are going to ram a truncheon up your hole until you confess to being a lunatic murderer.'

Peebles opened the door, relieved to see neither Miller nor Harry had their truncheons extended.

'Mr Kline, we'd like a word,' Harry said, standing just outside the trailer.

'Well, can it wait? My assistant director and I are going through some technical stuff.'

'No, it can't.'

'We can finish up going through the shooting script later, Randy,' Peebles said. Kline looked at him and stuck two fingers up.

'Right, you'd better come in.' Miller and Harry entered, followed by Charlie Meekle, who had reappeared as suddenly as he'd disappeared, citing bathroom issues.

'We'd just like to talk to you about Trisha Cornwall,' Harry said.

'Have a seat.' Peebles indicated for them to go through to the living room area.

Where? Harry thought. They glanced around then sat on the small settees on either side of the slide-outs. These were parts of the trailer that extended out to make the room more spacious.

'I was expecting you,' Kline said. 'You'll know by now that she was a stalker.'

'We do,' Meekle said. 'Looks like somebody wanted to shut her up.'

'Not me. She was nothing but a pain in the arse, but I wouldn't want that to happen to anybody.'

'We saw that she had texted you on the night she died.'

'She sent me a couple of texts,' Kline said, not denying it.

'Twenty-one, to be precise,' Harry said.

'A couple. Twenty-one. It's all the same. They got the same response; I told her I wasn't interested in seeing her again.'

'You slept with her,' Meekle said, his lip curling in disgust, 'then you told her to sod off.'

'We get a lot of groupies hanging about, believe it or not. They start out wanting an autograph of the stars, although describing them as stars is pushing it, but then they want to become friendly with the crew. They think that by sleeping with them, they'll get an introduction. The crew take advantage if you ask me. They know fine well that there's no chance of the stars going out with a fan.'

'But a director getting it away is always a possibility.'

'There's never any promise made or implied.'

'It doesn't seem that Trisha saw it that way,' Harry said.

'Trisha was her own worst enemy. She slept her way through the crew. They all talked about her. Don't get me wrong; she was an attractive woman, but it's what went on inside her head that made her daft.'

'Did she ever talk about Jill Thompson?' Meekle asked.

'Yes. She was Jill's best friend, back in the day.'

'Did you meet Trisha the night she died?'

'No. I told her she needed to calm down and to stop texting me. I was busy with the filming schedule, and it was over.'

'What about you, Mr Peebles?' Harry said. 'You ever meet Trisha?'

Peebles shifted position on his seat. 'Of course I did. She was never away from here. Always trying to get an autograph. When he knocked her back, she came to me, asking if I wanted to go for a drink. I told her to bog off.'

'How did she take that news?'

'She was pissed off, so she went back to annoying him.' He nodded at Kline.

'Yeah, thanks again for that, mate.'

'Where were you both last night?' Harry asked.

'Working here,' Kline said, 'then we went for a couple of beers, then I went to the hotel where we're all staying. Had some more drinks at the bar and went to my room.'

'I was with him, right up until we went to our separate rooms.'

'Where are you people based out of?' Meekle asked.

'Livingston. We used to have a studio here in Edinburgh, but it was getting too expensive. Now we have a place out in West Lothian.'

'Can you think of anybody else who Trisha was stalking?' Harry said.

'There was a member of the sound crew. She got her claws into him, bombarding him with Facebook messages, demanding to know why he didn't write back to her and questioning why he was talking to other women. Exactly the same way she was treating me. We were her personal toys and could only answer to her. He told her to sod off.'

Harry looked at him. 'Thank you for your time, Mr Kline. If you can think of anything else, give us a call.'

'He's using the script as his killing method,' Peebles said.

'What?' Harry said.

'The way those two women have been murdered? That's in the script. It's how God kills them, or the man who thinks he's God. The character has a God complex, deciding when they should leave Earth for Heaven. They have a problem in their life; he ends their life so the problem is solved, in his eyes.'

'How many people die in this script?' Meekle asked.

Kline paused for a minute. 'Seven.'

'Do you have a copy we can read?' Harry asked.

Kline walked across to a cupboard and took three copies out. 'Have one each. But do me a favour?'

'What?'

'Don't give one to that tosser Graham Balfour. He's already got two, both signed by some crew.'

The detectives left the trailer, knowing they had a blueprint to murder in their hands.

Mike Peebles made sure the police were out of earshot. 'Do you think they know?'

'How can they?' Kline said.

'Somebody might have told them.'

'Not much chance of that now, thank God.'

Peebles nodded. 'You got caught once. Twice was careless.'

'It will be fine, Mike. You'll see.'

'I hope for your sake you're right.'

TWENTY-FIVE

'Have you seen Weaver?' Harry said to Miller.

'Not since earlier.'

'God knows where he got to.' He watched Meekle get into a car and drive off. 'Keep your eye on him, Frank. He said we were going to exchange notes and he hasn't called me yet. He better be in my office first thing tomorrow or else he'll be back on the train heading south.'

'Will do.'

Harry waved Alex over. 'Frank and I are going to the Royal to see how Steffi Walker is doing. You want to come along?'

'Sure.'

Miller gave Hazel Carter the keys to their car. 'Tell me you know where that bus driver prick is,' he said.

'Not yet, sir. Sorry.'

They got in the car, Alex behind the wheel and headed up to the Royal Infirmary.

'Hanson's vanished off the face of the earth,' Miller said. 'Christ, I wish we knew where he was staying.'

The traffic was light and they made good time.

There were two officers guarding her room, different ones from earlier. They nodded to the detectives and stood aside.

Miller opened Steffi's door and stopped for an instant. 'Hey there,' he said.

She was looking at him, watching his eyes for a reaction.

'It looks a lot worse than it is,' she said, her voice sounding weak and hoarse. Her face was black and blue, the bruising having worsened throughout the day. Her head was wrapped in a bandage and she was still wired up to machines.

'Thank God it's only temporary,' Miller said. He mentally kicked himself for not seeing the signs when Steffi had had a mark on her face.

None of them asked her how she was feeling. They could see how she was feeling.

They made small talk for a little while.

'Listen, I don't want to put the wind up you, but we haven't found Hanson yet,' Harry said.

'I'm not pressing charges, sir,' she said.

'He's not going to stop, Steffi.'

'Have you heard from him?' Miller said.

'Christ, what is this? The three of you come in here and get my blood pressure up? It was a domestic and it got out of hand. He won't do it again.'

'We just want you to know we're here for you, Steffi,' Alex said, sitting down on the bed and holding her hand.

'I know that, but this is personal. He won't do it again.'

'Did he tell you that the time before, when you came to work with a mark on your face?' Miller said.

'Please don't take this the wrong way, sir, but would you all just please piss off?'

The two detectives looked around awkwardly for a moment.

'We care about you, Steff,' Miller said.

'I know, Frank, but I'm tired.'

And scared? he wanted to ask, but kept quiet.

'Why don't you two go and get a coffee. I'll meet you downstairs in the canteen,' Alex said, not budging from the bed.

Harry nodded and ushered Miller outside. They both heard Steffi starting to cry as they shut the door.

TWENTY-SIX

Later on, Harry McNeil sat on his couch with his feet up. He had brought files home from the office and was looking through them, trying to work out the puzzle.

His phone rang.

'Harry. Fancy a beer?'

Stan Weaver. Christ.

'Not tonight, Stan. I'm going through some papers.'

'Jesus, laddie, she's got you under the thumb and you're not even married.' He said it with a slight laugh but there was an undertone there.

'We're busy right now.' It was meant in a light tone but came out a bit more harsh than he'd wanted it to.

'Listen, about today-'

'I let that go, because you're going to retire, and you're probably stressed, and I've had a lot worse done to me, but if you ever talk to one of my team like that again—'

'*My* team!' Weaver shouted. 'They're still my team! And you'll what, Harry? Get your pals onto me? Well, here's a news flash; you haven't got any.'

There was silence between the two men and Harry could hear the background noise of the pub. Weaver was well on the way to getting blootered again. Then Harry heard another voice, like somebody was talking to Weaver.

'Don't take any guff off him. He pretends to be your pal, but there's a sleekit side to the wee bastard.'

Harry thought he recognised Meekle's voice, standing next to Weaver, egging him on. Not so wee, Harry thought but didn't correct Weaver's friend. 'Well, you have yourself a good night, Stan. Give Meekle my best.' He hung up as Weaver started calling him names.

He had just set his phone down when it buzzed. He thought it would be Vanessa, asking him again if he'd talked to Frank about the flat. *No, I haven't talked to him, alright?!*

This was the second of three nights of parents' meetings and Harry was glad. Not that he didn't enjoy Vanessa's company, but sometimes he just liked to be on his own for a wee while.

He huffed out his breath, annoyance starting to

grip him. *Why can't you just leave me alone for a little while?* He knew he shouldn't be thinking like this, but he just needed some space. To kick back and read a book. Or watch some Netflix. *Or read some death reports.*

He picked up his phone and read the message: *You eaten yet?*

Alex.

No. You? He put his finger over the send button and hesitated. Why had he immediately answered her? It had felt natural, like he was talking to a friend. That was one thing he liked about DS Maxwell; she was very easy to get on with and he was enjoying working with her.

Fancy a Chinese? My treat.

Come to think of it, he was hungry. He'd popped the tab on a can of lager and had some crisps with it. Now he was famished.

Lemon Chicken, fried rice plz. He hit send without any hesitation this time.

Fifteen minutes. Get the kettle on.

He sent her a smiley face. The last time he'd sent a text to his son, the boy had told him he needed to get with it, to use shortcuts when he was texting. He wondered what the shortcut for *fuck you* was. Not that he would use it with his son, but it might come in handy for Stan Weaver.

And then he felt the tiniest pang of guilt. Should he be doing this while his girlfriend was at her school, yakking to parents about how little Johnny is just wonderful, when all the time, little Johnny was a potential serial killer who thought nothing of cutting the curtains or drawing on the walls with crayons.

What is there to be guilty about, Harry? he asked himself. Working with a colleague? Everybody has to eat. And just because you're eating in your flat, is nothing to get jealous over.

Although, had it been Frank Miller who had suggested bringing the food over, he would have, not-quite-politely, declined.

Fifteen minutes in reality became twenty-five.

'Sorry I'm late,' Alex said when he opened his door to her. Her hair was wet from the sudden downpour that had started just minutes earlier. 'There was a queue. Who would have thought it would be so busy on a Tuesday night?'

He could see her shirt was wet as well. 'I could have come down and given you a hand,' he said, in the same way people said, *You shouldn't have done that* when they were tearing the wrapping off a birthday gift.

'It's fine,' she replied. 'You don't have a hairdryer, do you?'

'I do. Not for myself, but my girlfriend keeps one

here in case she stays over. Which is never, since she just lives across the road. In the cupboard under the bathroom sink. I'll dish up.'

She gave him the bag with the food and they stood awkwardly for a moment.

'I don't know where your bathroom is,' she said, smiling.

'Oh. Straight ahead.' They turned away from each other and a couple of minutes later, Harry could faintly hear the hairdryer going. He hoped she would dry her shirt too, instead of asking him for a bathrobe. Christ, that would be all he needed, for Vanessa to come home early and find another woman drying herself, like she'd just taken a shower.

His phone rang again. Vanessa's name was on the screen. 'Hello, he said, going through to the kitchen. *Please don't hear the hairdryer.*

'Hello, honey. Listen, I felt bad about not being there having dinner with you, so I thought I could bring something in if you don't mind eating a bit late?'

'Oh, don't worry about that. I fixed myself something. I wasn't that hungry, so I'll be fine. I'm just reading through some work stuff.'

He gently set the bag of food on the counter top, trying not to let it rustle.

'Are you at your own flat?'

He hesitated, looking for a loaded question. 'Yes.'

'Okay. I can come round and see you later.'

'Of course. I'll be here.' He looked at the clock; at least an hour and a half, maybe two hours before she got finished.

The sound of the hairdryer died.

'Right, I'll let you go. See you soon. Love you,' she said.

'Love you too,' he replied, and wondered, not for the first time, if he was just saying the words out of habit. He switched the kettle back on.

He'd hung up before Alex came into the kitchen, looking more presentable.

'I hope your girlfriend won't mind that I used her hairbrush too. I don't have nits.' She smiled.

'That's fine.' *Trust me, she'll never find out.*

They dished up the food and sat at the table in the living room, overlooking the bowling club, which had a lack of players. 'Rain stopped play,' he said, nodding down to the bowling green.

'I think that's cricket.'

'I know that, sergeant. It was merely an observation.' He smiled, not wanting her to think he was admonishing her.

'My ex used to like bowling.' She looked at him and laughed. 'Sorry. Every conversation won't be about my ex. It was just a thing he liked to do.'

They continued eating, washing the food down

with two cups of coffee. 'I was reading through the old case file,' he said.

'Anything pop out?'

'One thing; they filmed in the cemetery for just over a week last time. Nine, ten days, something like that. Exactly the same timeframe for this part of the shoot, but there was only one murder. Why have there been two murders this time?'

'Different killers, would be the obvious answer.'

'But is it? I'm thinking that maybe it's not. Something about this stupid show is making this guy kill women connected to it, but I was checking; the two victims now weren't connected to the first show twenty years ago. The only connection is Trisha Cornwall lived near there before her family moved to London, and she would hang around the cemetery with the others.'

Alex nodded. 'Why was Jill Thompson killed twenty years ago? The connection is the show itself; they were filming the first one back then, and as soon as filming starts on the remake, a killer strikes again. Somebody with a grudge?'

'Could be. I'll get the team to co-ordinate with Miller's team and see who was there the last time.'

They ate in silence for a few moments, and Harry's heart missed a beat when he thought he saw Vanessa's car turn into their street.

'Does your girlfriend know I'm here?' Alex asked, as if reading his mind.

'How could she? She's working late.'

'We have things called mobile phones these days, Harry.'

'It's Chief Inspector.'

'Sorry, sir.'

He shook his head at her smiling. 'Should have seen your face.'

'Touché. But tell me a little bit about yourself.'

'It's not very interesting.'

'Tell me anyway.' She put her knife and fork on the plate and finished her coffee.

'Well, I was married young, and I have a fifteen-year-old son. I got divorced, ex-wife and son moved to Fife to be near her family. In Kelty, where we were today. Her brother hates me, and we got into an altercation one day, and I battered him after he attacked me, and I've never seen any of her family again. I go and see my son every couple of weeks. He's a great kid, but being poisoned against me by the wicked witch from the north.'

He finished his own meal and sat and stared out of the window for a moment, thinking back ten years to when his boy was just little. Good times.

He turned to look at her.

'Now tell me a little bit about yourself. I already

know you were engaged and your ex dumped you and you sold your flat and moved to the colonies. In fact, I know most things there are to know about you.'

'Oh, this is like going on a dating site. Not that I would know, mind, but I've heard some of the others talking about it.'

'Yeah, sure you have.'

'When I first met you yesterday, you didn't strike me as being annoying,' Alex said, 'but now I'm going to re-evaluate my opinion of you.'

He laughed. 'Carry on.'

'Like you, my life story isn't very exciting. I left school and wanted to join the police, so I was over the moon when Lothian and Borders accepted my application. I worked my way into CID, became a sergeant and belted the Lord Provost's son. The rest you know.'

'I don't know what your boyfriend did for a living.'

'He's a fireman. Fire*fighter*. I came home one day and found him giving a fireman's lift to a female recruit in our bedroom. We went our own way after that. Five years ago.'

'That must have been tough.'

'Not as tough as Gregg losing his wife and child.'

'True.'

They cleared the dishes and sat in the living room, going over the case.

'It all boils down to the *why* as you said. Why

would anybody want to kill people connected with the show?'

'I think we can rule out an irate fan.'

'We need to try and find out who the father of Jill Thompson's baby was.'

'Do you think it was Randy Kline?' Alex said, some of the notes on her lap.

'If it was, he's certainly not saying.'

They carried on reading, Harry keeping an eye on the clock.

TWENTY-SEVEN

The doctor walked with confidence along the corridor and turned right towards the room. Two police officers were standing guard.

'Give me a shout if you need a coffee and I'll have somebody bring you one,' he said with a smile to the officers.

They nodded as he took his stethoscope off and opened the door. Nobody else was in the room.

Steffi Walker was sleeping as the doctor lifted the chart. He didn't know what he was looking at. After all, he'd only been a doctor for ten minutes.

Peter Hanson put the chart back and stood looking at Steffi. He knew he didn't have long before the officers outside would wonder what he was doing and come in to investigate.

So he woke her up. By pinching her arm.

'Wakey, wakey, sleeping beauty.' He nipped and twisted the skin on her upper arm. She woke with a start and Hanson released his grip.

'You must have been in a deep sleep. Were you dreaming of me?' He smiled at her, his face full of malice.

'What are you doing here? How did you get in?' Then she saw the doctor's coat he was wearing and the stethoscope.

'I wanted to see you, but they all think I'm a monster, Steffi. I mean, I know I lost my temper, I admit that.' He took a step back and held his hands up. 'But I've thought about it, and how stupid I was. I mean, really, really stupid. God, I lifted my hand to the woman I love. What kind of a fool does that make me?'

'You need to go, Peter. It won't look good for you if they catch you in here.'

'They won't let me explain, that's for sure. That's why I wanted to see you in private. Steffi, I love you and I'm sorry for what I did. It won't ever happen again. I don't know what came over me.'

'You need help.'

'I know and I'll get help. I'll go and see somebody. I promise. I just want us to start afresh.' He looked at her face, saw the tears streaming down her cheeks. 'I want to come home.'

'I don't know. You hurt me.'

'It won't ever happen again.'

'You said that the last time, Peter. You begged me for another chance. I gave it to you.'

'It was a mistake. It won't ever happen again, I promise you. I love you, Steffi.' He leant over and kissed her. 'Can I come home?'

She hesitated for a second before answering. 'Yes.'

'Thank you.' He turned to look at the door. 'I need to go before they wonder what's going on. I love you. Call me when you're leaving the hospital and I'll come home to you.'

As he turned and made for the door she asked him, 'Where are you staying?' but he opened the door and slipped out without answering.

TWENTY-EIGHT

'Don't worry,' Rita Mellon said to her boyfriend, Brian. 'I'll be fine.'

'It's not you I'm worried about. I mean, we don't even know this guy, yet here you are, going out for dinner with him.'

Rita finished putting her lipstick on and adjusted her bra through her blouse. 'He's sound if he knows Adrian.'

'I suppose. But what if he takes a fancy to you?'

She laughed. 'Brian, love, I've been around other men before. I can spot a letch a mile off. I have managed to interact with men in the past without sleeping with them! What do you think I did when I was married to Malkie?'

Mad Malkie Mellon was Rita's ex-husband whose

current abode was the Bar-L, a notorious Glaswegian prison, formally known as Barlinnie.

'I wish you wouldn't mention him,' Brian said, sipping at his whisky. He was a good bit younger than Rita, but the two of them were inseparable.

'I can't pretend I wasn't married to him. Besides, Adrian assured me that somebody over there has had a word with Malkie and he won't ever be giving me trouble again.'

'Very reassuring, but I still worry about you.'

'Come here,' she said to him, turning away from the mirror in the living room. She gave him a hug. 'No kiss; I've just put my lippie on.'

'I suppose a quickie before you go is out of the question?'

She playfully slapped his arm. 'He's waiting downstairs for me.'

'Be good,' Brian said as she left the apartment and took the lift down to the lobby. She loved living here with Brian and was grateful to Adrian Jackson for providing the flat for them. If he wasn't married and Brian wasn't his nephew, then maybe...

Downstairs, she looked around for the car, but none was there. No flashy motor anyway. Then she got a text. *Damn car broke down! Could you get an Uber to the restaurant? So sorry! Harvey's in Leith.*

She texted back that it would be fine. She thought about going back upstairs but then Brian might think this was her fault and insist on coming along. She could handle this, and this investor was important to Adrian. Theo had told her in confidence that Adrian was having doubts about this project, but if he, Theo, got on board, they could make a killing with the merchandising.

She didn't want to mess this up for Adrian.

She got an Uber five minutes later.

Theo was waiting outside the restaurant for her. He was a fit-looking man, maybe in his forties, but he looked like he worked out. He had slick hair and a dark shadow on his face, like no matter how many times a day he shaved, he would always have this five o'clock shadow.

'Rita?' he said as she stepped out of the car.

'Yes.' She smiled at him. His handshake was firm and dry.

'I must apologise again. I really don't know what's wrong with the car. It's a classic car but recently she seems to be playing up. I need to buy a new one. I'm awfully embarrassed.'

'Think nothing of it.' She looked at the restaurant. It was closed.

'I can't believe this place is gone. I know somebody who invested in it.' He looked at her. 'The *Blue*

Martini is just along the way. We can get a table there, I'm sure.'

He ushered her inside and they were shown to a table that Theo had booked days earlier.

They made small talk until they each had a glass of wine and had placed their orders. Then he took his phone out and switched it off. 'I think it's just rude when people are in a business meeting and their phone goes off. There's a time and a place, and having a financial meeting isn't one of them.'

'Oh, yes. I agree.' Rita took her own phone out and switched it off.

'I'll switch it back on later, but right now, it helps one to clear the mind and deal with the matter at hand.'

'Absolutely.'

Their food came and Rita thought it smelled magnificent.

'Once again, I contacted you directly, as Adrian had mentioned he had you on board and you were the brains of the outfit. He was getting the jitters, so to speak. We had a meeting and I mentioned that me and my partners might be interested in coming aboard. And to be honest, after I read about the original show, I was hooked. Of course, I then remembered when it came out and how successful it was. This time, we can hit America with it, big time. You see, the one big advantage we have now is streaming TV, like Netflix.'

Rita smiled and nodded at the appropriate times. She had a feeling the deal was already done, and Theo just wanted to spend some time with her.

'So, what do you say?' he asked her. 'Does it sound like a plan? Us coming on board?'

'I don't see why not. I'll talk with Adrian and he can get the financial side of things worked out with his team of accountants.'

'Great. As I said, I think Adrian just needs that little push. Now, what do you say we order some champagne?'

'Oh, I'm not sure. I don't usually drink much.'

'Listen, this dinner is a business expense, and it would be absolutely remiss of me to not have at least one bottle at the table.'

'Go on then.'

Theo smiled and indicated for the waiter and he came back with the bottle.

'As long as I don't end up dead drunk,' she said.

Just dead, he thought, and they clinked glasses.

TWENTY-NINE

'Of all the fucking stupid things you've done, this one has bells on it,' Adrian Jackson said, pacing about Brian's living room. 'Just as well I called.'

'I didn't know, for Christ's sake. Rita was dealing with this because this guy had her convinced that she was doing you a favour by talking directly to him.'

'What exactly did she say?' He had taken his bowler hat off but was still using the walking stick.

'She said they had been talking. He wanted to discuss investing in the show as everybody stood to make a lot of money, but you were getting cold feet. He said they should talk over dinner.'

Jackson stopped the pacing. 'Try her again.'

Brian called Rita's number and it went straight to voicemail. 'Nothing. It's dead.'

'Let's hope she's not.'

'Don't talk like that, Adrian, for God's sake.'

'Go through everything that happened tonight, again.' Jackson sat down.

'She said he had texted her and he would pick her up downstairs. She left, and then she said he had sent her a text that his car had broken down and she had got an Uber. I tried sending her a text a little while ago but got no answer. I wanted to call her, just to see that she was safe, but her phone was off.'

'This is a nightmare.'

'Are you sure you're not dealing with another investor?' Brian said.

'Of course I'm bloody well sure. We don't need other investors in on this. Are you daft?' He stood up again. 'Molloy is going to go off his fucking nut. I'll need to call him.'

'I called Uber and they wouldn't tell me where she went. Privacy and all that.'

'Fuck that for a game of soldiers.' He called Robert Molloy and explained the situation.

'Get yourself round here, Adrian. I'm at the hotel.'

'I'll be right round. Five minutes.' He hung up. Molloy was at *the hotel* which meant his hotel on North Bridge, the one he owned with his son.

'Come on, Brian, and for God's sake, let me do the

talking. We don't want Michael Molloy acting like he's on crack. When he's in one of his moods, people usually start losing body parts, especially if they've shagged him out of money. Stay calm, and if you *do* have to talk, just look like you're an idiot. Which shouldn't be too hard for you.'

THIRTY

The champagne had tasted good, she had to admit. But she made a point of not getting drunk. She didn't want Brian to get the wrong idea when she got home. But it had gone straight to her head.

'How about we go along and have a look round the set now?' he said to her.

They were standing outside. It was dark and cold now, a breeze coming in from the Forth just across the way.

'It's a bit dark to be messing about in a cemetery don't you think?'

'I know it's dark, but the film crew will be there. It's not as if they all go home for the night and leave all the stuff. Besides, I heard them talking and they said they were filming in there tonight, so there's going to be plenty of people about. What do you say? Maybe we'll get an autograph or two.'

'Oh, okay then. But I want you to take a photo of me there so I can show my boyfriend.'

'Deal.'

She giggled to herself. Her head was swimming a little bit.

'That champagne must have been strong.'

'It was an eighty-two' he said, as if he knew what he was talking about. He figured Rita wouldn't know the difference between a bottle of champagne and a bottle of shampoo.

'Rita?' he said.

She looked at him.

He pointed to a white van that was parked just past the restaurant. 'It's all I could get at short notice. A friend of mine is a builder and he let me borrow it.'

She hesitated for a moment but the champagne had loosened her inhibitions just a bit. Enough to accept a lift in a van.

'Oh, I suppose so.' Rita climbed into the Transit, hoping she wouldn't get her clothes dirty, but it looked clean.

It was an unusually clean van, nothing like she'd expected the inside of a builder's van to look. Theo got in and they drove away from the shore. He headed up towards Warriston.

He drove past the crematorium and parked outside the side gate. 'There's security so we'll have to be careful,' he said.

'Why can't we just drive through the main gate?'

'What with the murders, they've tightened up security. They might not let us on the set. But I want you to experience it.' He jumped out of the van and walked across to the gate. She got out on unsteady feet.

'It's padlocked,' Rita said.

'I've never met a padlock yet that couldn't be broken, Rita.'

That's when Rita got the bad feeling. She was standing looking at the gate when she turned around and saw Theo coming at her with the polythene bag in his hand.

It was instinct for her to scream. Which she did, loud and long.

Theo rushed her and put the polythene bag over her head. She struggled against him, but he was too powerful for her. He started to drag her back to the van.

Rita reached up to his face and dug her nails in, feeling something come away.

She didn't hear the other man shouting, but Theo did.

'Oy! What are you doing?' The man was standing further up, near the gates to the crematorium.

'You want some of this?' Theo shouted back.

'I'll give you some of *this*, ya bastard!' the man said, then Theo saw the German Shepherd he had with him. The man started walking towards him, and the dog started barking and snarling.

'Let her go or I'll set the fucking dog on you!'

Theo watched as the man bent down to unclip the lead. He weighed up his options; try and get Rita into the van, quicker than the dog could run down here, or cut his losses.

Guessing how fast the dog would be, he pushed Rita roughly away from him and jumped into the van and drove away. He looked in the mirror and saw the man hadn't let the dog go, but was running towards Rita, the dog's lead in one hand, a mobile phone in the other. Theo didn't put the lights on so the man couldn't see the license plate. Only when he got over the bridge into the other side of Warriston Road did he risk the lights.

'Too bad, Rita, we could have had a good thing going. I had the very gravestone picked out that was going to crush your skull into pieces, but never mind. There's always next time.'

THIRTY-ONE

Robert Molloy was sitting behind his desk, a glass of brandy in his hand. His Rottweiler – otherwise known as his son, Michael – was also there, which didn't surprise Jackson. He gave Brian a quick look, reminding him of the lecture he'd given him about not upsetting Michael.

'Adrian. I wish I could say I was pleased to see you,' Robert said, 'but considering the circumstances...'

'What's this about some fuck trying to get one over on us?' Michael said, getting straight to the point.

'Brian here told me that somebody conned my assistant Rita into believing he was an investor.'

'Where is she now?' he asked, his face like thunder, gritting his teeth.

'That's the thing; we don't know. Uber won't tell us where they took her.'

'Won't they now?' Robert said. 'And this person knows who he's fucking with?'

'Apparently not,' Jackson said.

'Indeed, or the thought would never cross his mind.' He looked at Michael. 'Have somebody get the information we need. Hack into whatever it takes to find out where Rita went. Then find this bastard. Teach him a lesson he'll never forget.'

'We just need to obtain some information about him.'

'I'm sure Mrs Mellon will oblige when we see her.'

Just then Brian's phone rang. 'What? Oh fuck, no. Is she alright?' he listened to the voice on the other end. 'We'll be right there.' He hung up and looked at Jackson.

'It's Rita; she was attacked and she's in the Royal.'

'What? Is she okay?' Jackson said.

'Yes. They're checking her over.'

Robert stood up. 'Michael, get my driver. We're going to the hospital. Then get a team together. I want that fucker hunted down. No expense spared. If he thinks he's going to fuck with the Molloys, I'll have that carved on his face before we put him in the ground.' He looked at Jackson as Michael left the office. 'You got your car?'

'My driver's downstairs.'

'See you at the Royal.'

THIRTY-TWO

Harry McNeil heard a noise and couldn't figure out what it was. It was his phone ringing, playing a stupid tune he didn't know the name of. He'd dozed off on the couch, watching some show that was being repeated.

He felt groggy; his eyes tired. The phone was doing the fandango on the table, vibrating its way across to the edge. It almost made the leap before he caught it.

'McNeil.'

'Harry, it's Frank Miller. We've got a situation. A woman was attacked.'

Harry paused for a second. 'What's that got to do with us?'

'She was attacked by the cemetery gates down in Warriston Road. He tried to get her to go into the cemetery. Can you come up to the Royal? I think it was our guy.'

'I'll be there as soon as. I'll leave in a few.'

As he got up, he looked at the clock. Well after eleven. He was relieved that Vanessa hadn't called or come round. Then he felt disappointed that she hadn't. *Make up your mind, Harry.*

'You dressed?' Harry asked Alex Maxwell. 'And before you come out with a smart reply, we have another possible victim. This one survived. I got a call to go to the Royal. I thought you'd like to tag along.'

'I am, and I can leave in two minutes. I'll see you up there. Unless...?'

'I'll be waiting downstairs.' He put his shoes on and brushed his teeth before going downstairs to wait on Alex.

He was glad she didn't honk her car horn again. He looked over to Vanessa's house, halfway up the hill, diagonally across the bowling green, and saw a bedroom light on. He felt a pang of something; guilt?

The passenger window rolled down. 'This will be a lot quicker if you actually get in the car, sir.'

He opened the BMW's door and got in and had barely buckled his seatbelt before she floored it.

'*Sir,* now? I can't see this new you lasting long. Showing me respect and stuff.'

She grinned at him. 'Me neither.'

'I knew it. I should mark it in my diary. We'll call it the *Maxwell showing respect* holiday. People all over Scotland will be celebrating.'

She hit the top of the street and turned up towards Queensferry Road, making it without having to wait for traffic at this time of night. She cut through the city centre and went up Lothian Road to cut through The Meadows.

Harry was lost in his own thoughts as Alex tuned in to a radio station that was playing tunes Harry didn't even know the names of.

THIRTY-THREE

Miller was waiting for Harry in the accident and emergency department. Stan Weaver and Charlie Meekle had also turned up.

'Tell me what this has to do with our case, Frank,' Harry said. He hadn't bothered fiddling with a tie.

'Her name's Rita Mellon. She's been taken up to a ward and we have somebody guarding her room. Come on, I'll tell you on the way.'

They walked through to the lift, Weaver and Meekle following. 'It seems she met the guy, who had told her he was an investor. They had dinner, and he drove her to the cemetery in a van, saying they could look around the film set.'

'I'm assuming this guy has nothing to do with financing the show?' Alex said to Harry as they stepped into the lift and hit the button for the second floor. He was ignoring the other two detectives. If they wanted a fight in the lift, Harry was in the right frame of mind.

'Nothing. Nobody knows who he is.'

'She's lucky to be alive. How did she get away from him?' Meekle asked.

They stepped out onto the second floor and walked along the hallway to where Rita Mellon's ward was.

'She screamed and the crematorium manager – who lives on the premises – was out with his German Shepherd and he saw the guy attacking her. He threatened him with the dog, and the attacker fled in a van,' Miller said.

'Did he get the number?' As Weaver asked, Harry could swear he smelled drink on the older DCI again.

'No. He drove away with the lights off. But get this; Rita got some of the guy's face.'

Harry stopped. 'What do you mean, *his face*?'

'She tried to scratch him but got some latex instead. The bastard had put a mask on, but not like the kind you would buy in a shop. This was like the kind that would be put on by an actor.'

'Christ, do you think it could have some DNA on it?'

'It's already away to the lab.'

Miller slowed down a bit. 'Adrian Jackson and the

Molloys are here. Rita is Jackson's nephew's live-in girlfriend.'

'We don't need them milling about here.' Harry looked at Adrian Jackson as they approached the private ward that Rita was in.

'Any news, Inspector?' Jackson asked.

'Not yet. We need to ask Mrs Mellon some more questions.' He turned to Harry. 'This is DCI McNeil. He's working with us on this enquiry.'

'We're going to need all the details about how Mrs Mellon came to be going out with this man for dinner,' Harry said.

'Anything you need.'

They went into the room. Brian was sitting with Rita.

'We meet again, Brian, or should I say, Mr Wellington?' Miller said, referring to Brian's *business* name of Carruthers Wellington.

'Inspector Miller.'

'Give us a minute, son,' Harry said to him.

'Please catch the bastard who did this to her.' Brian squeezed Rita's hand before getting up from the chair and leaving.

'I'm fine, really,' Rita said.

'They just want to check you out, Rita,' Miller said. 'There's a lot of people worrying about you.'

'That's nice, but I just got a fright. The bastard put

a polythene bag over my head.' Her lip started to tremble a bit. 'He tried to kill me.'

'You're safe now. We'll have officers posted here, outside your door, but I'm sure Adrian will have people close by too. He's not going to get you.'

'Thank God for that man with his dog. He saved my life.'

Miller sat on the edge of the bed while Harry sat on the chair. Weaver and Meekle stood around like a couple of wallflowers at the local singles club. Alex stood well away from them.

'Tell us from the beginning about how you ended up going to dinner with him.'

She did and they listened.

'What about the van? Anything distinctive about it?' Weaver asked.

'No, well, yes; in a way. It was clean. I mean, spotless. Like he'd been on his hands and knees with a scrubbing brush, cleaning it. He said his car had broken down and he borrowed this van from a friend, who was a builder. But that was no builder's van. Not a speck of dust on it. But listen to me; I thought he was some high-flying finance guy, and he had a bloody van. More fool me.'

'From what we know about him, he's very clever, and very convincing.'

'Is there anything that sticks out about him?' Alex

asked.

'No. He was charming, but he did go on about the first *God Complex*. He said it was a wasted opportunity. I thought that sounded strange because it was a very famous show. A wasted opportunity for what?'

A knowing look passed between Harry and Miller; *He could have killed more people.*

'You grabbed his face and a piece came off,' Harry said.

'Yes. It was like he had a rubber face. He didn't scream or anything, and there was no blood, but it was like he had put on a disguise.'

They asked her a few more questions but it was clear she didn't know much more.

Outside, Miller looked at the others. 'It's somebody who's working for that production company. He would know how to put a face on.'

'Agreed,' Weaver said. 'We'll get a full list of names tomorrow. By then we should have a positive ID on the second victim. If it is indeed Aileen Rogers, then we know she was a make-up artist on the set.'

'Maybe she was doing make-up on our killer. Maybe she found out and he had to kill her,' Meekle said.

'First thing tomorrow, I want a list of people who work there, and I want them re-interviewed,' Harry said.

'I'll make sure we have it first thing,' Miller told him.

Miller saw Robert Molloy approaching.

'I'll get off, Frank. See you in the morning.' Harry rapidly caught up with the other two detectives as they walked away to where Alex was standing close by.

'What's up, McNeil?' Weaver said.

'I'm telling you this to your face; you ever call me up at home and talk to me like that again, I'll break your jaw. And you, Meekle, egging him on. You need him to fight your battles?'

Meekle took a step forward but Weaver put an arm out to stop him. 'Listen to you; you've got a pair of balls after all.'

'In my time with Standards, I've fought a lot harder men than you. Both of you. Pair of bastards.'

Weaver grinned. 'See what you're getting into, Maxwell? Having a boss like him?'

'Better than having a boss like you.'

The smile fell from Weaver's face. 'You watch your mouth.'

'Or else what?'

He sneered at her. 'I reckon that firefighter boyfriend of yours got a lucky escape.' He and Meekle turned away.

'That cheeky—'

Harry put his hands on her arms. 'Forget him. He's not worth it.'

She sagged and let out a breath. 'When I told you Weaver was alright to work with, I lied; he's made my life hell.'

'I thought as much. Come on, you can drive me home.'

'That's the best offer I'm going to get tonight.' She smiled weakly as they walked in the opposite direction from Weaver.

Molloy reached Miller.

'Well, well, Harry McNeil isn't dead after all. I haven't seen that scrote for ages. Or that other balloon, Weaver.' He watched as Harry disappeared into the lift.

'He's not too bad.'

'Compared to what?' Molloy shook his head and made a face. 'Who's the other one?'

'Charlie Meekle. He's up from Newcastle.'

Molloy shook his head. 'Anyway, I heard that one of your officers is in here.'

'Yes. Steffi Walker.'

'She's such a nice lassie.'

'Somebody gave her a kicking.'

'I hope you got the bastard.'

'We did and we didn't,' Miller said.

'Stop talking in riddles.'

'It was a domestic. Her boyfriend gave her a doing.'

'Jesus. And she's a copper, too. I hope you gave him a slap in the cells.'

'Come on now, Molloy. You know we don't operate like that, as much as we'd sometimes like to.'

'So he's going to get, what? A slap on the wrist from one of those ponces on the bench?'

'We don't even have him yet, but even if we do get him, Steffi isn't pressing charges.'

'He'll walk, in other words.'

'That's the bottom line.'

Molloy shook his head. 'You know, her and that other lassie, Julie, they took on a killer who was hell bent on killing me and they overpowered him. No hesitation. They saved my life that night. And now some fuck has hit her and he's going to get a tickle from some old wiggy judge? That's a fucking sin, Frank.'

'We have to abide by the law.'

'That's true. *You* do.'

'Behave yourself, Molloy,' Miller said, but there was no conviction in his tone.

'I have no choice. I don't know his name or where he works.'

Miller had an idea Molloy knew *exactly* who Peter Hanson was and where he worked. He looked over Molloy's shoulder and saw Julie Stott further along the white corridor, looking at them. Then she was gone.

THIRTY-FOUR

Graham Balfour had just settled in for the night when there was a gentle tap at his door. 'Christ, you're late,' he said, roughly pulling the door open.

A masked man pushed him, Balfour fell on his back and the big man towered over him.

'Get up,' the man said.

'What the hell do you think you're doing?' Balfour said, getting to his feet. 'I'm calling the police.' He pulled his phone out of his pocket and the man slapped it out of Balfour's hand before stepping over the threshold and closing the door behind him.

Balfour tried to fight back then a gloved fist punched him in the face. 'Shout and I'll fucking kill you.'

The big man grabbed his hair and dragged him

through to the living room and threw him down onto the couch.

'Answer my questions and maybe I won't kill you,' he said.

'What? What the fuck are you talking about?' Balfour was scared now and barely holding onto his sphincter muscle.

'You heard. You're not fucking daft, are you? Although you pretend to be.'

'Listen, I don't know what's going on, but you need to leave.'

'I'm going to as soon as you tell me what I want to know.'

'Which is?'

'Who killed Trisha Cornwall?'

'I don't know. I swear.'

'Oh, I think you do know. And now he's killing other people. But I want him first. Was it you?'

'No, it wasn't me. Of course it wasn't me.'

The big man glowered at him. 'Who was messing with Jill Thompson? Who put his hands on a little girl?'

Balfour sat up straighter. 'I really don't know.'

The man stood chewing the inside of his cheek for a moment, then suddenly, like a cobra striking its victim, he lashed out, punching Balfour again. Then he grabbed his hair.

'People think you're special needs, that you lived with mummy and daddy because you're daft and couldn't get a job. So now you sign on, and make money from selling autographs. Utter pish. You don't fool me, Balfour. You're fucking at it. How do you really make money?'

'We sell stuff, honest.'

'Don't talk shite.' He punched Balfour again, then pulled him to his feet by the hair.

'Please don't hurt me.'

'How do you make money?'

'We steal their stuff and sell it on a black website. People will pay a lot of money for some of that stuff, especially... underwear. Not clean underwear.'

'Dirty bastard. Was Trisha Cornwall part of this?'

'Yes, but she would meet with some of them and sleep with them and take photos.'

The man shook his head. 'And blackmail them?'

'Yes.'

'Now we're getting somewhere.'

'This is all her fault. A grown woman for fuck's sake. She couldn't control herself though and she started getting nasty. I wish I'd never met her.'

'Did you kill her?' the man asked again.

'Of course not. I slept with her, but I didn't kill her.'

'She let you touch her?' the man said, his voice full of scepticism.

'I'll show you.' He got up and left the room for a moment, coming back in with a pair of women's knickers. 'Some people will pay a lot of money for these; underwear from a murder victim.'

'You disgust me,' the man said, snatching the flimsy garment and putting it in his pocket.

'Hey, those are mine.'

'Not now.' The man was inches from Balfour. 'What happened back then? To Jill.'

'I have no idea. She seemed obsessed with one of the crew.'

'Which one?'

'I don't know,' Balfour said, 'but she was in love with him.'

'Do you think he killed her?'

'Who knows? But what if he got her pregnant, and thought he did the best thing by getting rid of her. It would have ruined him after all. She was a little slag, by all accounts.' Balfour looked into the eyes of the man and saw nothing. Like he was staring into the past.

'What did you call her?' he said, his voice barely a whisper.

'A slag,' Balfour said. 'She got what was coming to her.'

'So will you...' The man punched Balfour in the

face, bursting his nose. 'Do you know who killed Trisha?'

Balfour couldn't speak; rolling about on the floor holding his nose.

'I know you know who killed her. I'll be back.'

Then the man calmly walked out of the living room and quietly closed the front door behind him.

THIRTY-FIVE

'You look tired this morning,' Alex said to Harry McNeil as she pulled the pool car into the car park at the back of the station in the high street.

'The last thing I expected was to get called out to the Royal.' He unclipped his seatbelt and rolled the window up. Even fresh air hadn't gotten rid of the stale unpleasant smell inside the vehicle.

'I swear to God, those lazy sods in the pool garage better take a vacuum cleaner to this thing tonight.'

'We could always use your wee Honda,' Alex said, smiling at him over the roof. 'Do you have dice hanging from the mirror?'

'Your attempt at humour is falling on deaf ears.'

Upstairs, Frank Miller was standing in front of the whiteboard. 'Morning, sir,' he said.

'How's things, Frank?'

'We got word back from the lab that what Rita Mellon pulled off her attacker was indeed synthetic material used on TV. It's painted on. Easy to apply, if you know what you're doing.'

'Where's Weaver and Meekle?'

'I haven't seen them this morning.'

'Listen up!' Percy Purcell came into the room. 'The family of Aileen Rogers was notified last night about the possible death of their daughter, and her dental records have just been checked, confirming her identity. We have to go and speak with the husband.'

Purcell spoke again. 'The lab is trying to see if they can get DNA off the piece of mask that Mrs Mellon pulled off the attacker's face.'

'Any leads on the van, boss?' one of the younger detectives asked.

'Nothing. A white Transit van, that's all we got. We're checking CCTV in the area.'

Purcell walked over to Miller. 'On Trisha Cornwall's phone were numbers for Graham Balfour and Randy Kline. We also identified another number; Aileen Rogers. She had spoken to Trish on the night of her death.'

'They all knew each other?' Harry said.

'Well, they're connected; Balfour was a friend of Trisha's. Now we know Trisha was connected to Aileen Rogers, and both women are dead.'

'I don't believe this nonsense that Balfour and his little gang make money selling autographs and the like,' Harry said. 'I mean, they might do, but I can't see them making much money from them.'

One of the junior detectives answered a ringing phone then shouted for Purcell. 'Sir, Commander Bridge would like a word in her office. Inspectors Miller and McNeil to be in attendance also.'

Purcell looked at them. 'Gentlemen, let's not keep the lady waiting.'

Upstairs in her office, Jeni Bridge was holding a piece of paper in her hand which she handed over to Purcell.

'Remember I said we would have Jill Thompson's DNA checked again from the samples we had from 1999? The results are back in.' She looked at Miller and McNeil then back to Purcell. Handed him the piece of paper.

'Go get him.'

THIRTY-SIX

Robert Molloy walked along the corridor, his body-guard holding two bunches of flowers. He stopped at Rita's door and knocked.

She was pleased to see him and accepted the flowers. There was a bruise on her face from where the attacker had hit her.

'How are you feeling today, Mrs Mellon?'

'Better, Mr Molloy, thank you. And thank you for the flowers. They're beautiful.'

'Call me Robert. We're all one big family now. We look after each other. And that's what I wanted to talk to you about.'

'Oh yes?'

'Yes. This man who took you to dinner last night; did you tell the police anything that might help catch him?'

'I told them everything I knew. Why? Was that wrong?'

'No, of course not. We need to get him, Rita, and I don't care if it's us or the police. As long as he's caught. But did he tell you anything that might have stuck out?'

'He was very charming. He said he had a classic car and that it had broken down, but I don't believe that now. I was surprised when he said we were getting into a van.'

'It was a white Transit?'

'Yes.'

'Which way did he go when you left the restaurant?'

'We drove past the bars at the shore then we turned right into Commercial Street and headed up to Ferry Road.'

Molloy nodded then made small talk for a little bit before standing up. 'I have to stop by and see somebody else. Two of my people are outside and will be there in shifts until it's time for you to leave, then Adrian will make sure you're safe.'

'Thank you for coming here, Robert. It means a lot.'

He leant over and kissed her cheek. Then he left and walked along the corridor, his man now carrying one bunch of flowers.

Molloy told a nurse he was there to visit a friend of

the family. The two policemen stood aside to let him enter with the flowers.

'Hello, DS Walker. I'm here visiting a friend and I thought these might cheer you up.'

'Hello. That's very kind.'

Molloy's eyes went to the bruising on Steffi's face as she sniffed the bouquet. He took them back and put them on a table.

'It seems you've been having a bit of a to-do with your boyfriend.' She started to protest but he held up a hand.

'Please indulge an old man.'

She settled back on the bed.

'Steffi, let me tell you a little story; my girlfriend, Jean, has been married before. She thought her husband was the love of her life. She even took his little boy as her own, before she and her husband had a little girl, God rest her soul. But although the husband was kind at first, as soon as they got comfortable, he would hit her. Just a little slap at first, then they got harder. And he would apologise and promise her it would never happen again.

'Until the next time. He would hit her again, and harder this time, and the frequency increased. He would hit her harder and there would be less time between these assaults. Until she'd had enough. It was hard for her, but she had to leave him. And only then did it stop.'

'Do you have a point, Mr Molloy?'

'It's not going to stop, Steffi. It's going to get worse. Why am I here talking to you like this? Because you and Julie Stott saved my life that night, I have no doubt. You are a very brave young woman, and I have a soft spot for you. I like you and I can't say that about a lot of coppers.'

'I'll be fine.'

'Be honest with me; has he managed to sneak in and see you?'

She was silent for a moment. 'How did you know?'

'It's what they do. They are master manipulators. Did he come dressed as a doctor?'

'Yes.'

'It's the logical thing. Frank Miller would go off his nut if he found out. Not at you, but Hanson.'

'Please don't tell him,' she pleaded.

'I'm not going to. Let me leave you with this though; he promised you it wouldn't happen again and you could start fresh. He will never hurt you again and he's sorry for what happened.'

She stayed silent.

Molloy stood looking down at her. 'They're false promises, Steffi. Just bear that in mind.' He saw tears running down her cheeks.

'I don't want to end up alone,' Steffi said.

'You won't. You can find somebody else, somebody who will love you without resorting to hitting you when things get a little rough.'

'I used to be in the army. I'm a detective. I'm not supposed to feel this scared, Mr Molloy. But I am. I can see something lurking in his eyes. I've seen it there before, in people that I've arrested: evil.' She looked him right in the eyes. 'This is something I can't tell Frank, but I'm scared. I have nobody else to tell that to.'

Steffi started sobbing and Molloy put an arm around her.

'You've got me,' he said.

And when he left her a little while later, he called his son. 'Get somebody up to the Royal. I want some men standing outside a couple of doors. And also, there's one other little thing I want taken care of.'

When he was done, he left the hospital.

THIRTY-SEVEN

'I hope Vanessa didn't give you too much of a hard time last night when she got home and found out you had Chinese with me,' Alex said as she drove down North Bridge behind the other unmarked cars.

'If this is blackmail, it isn't going to work.'

'Oh dear, what a mind you have. I was just hoping that she's not the jealous type.'

'That's none of your business, sergeant.'

Alex smiled.

'Let me ask you something,' Harry said. 'Did you drive Weaver out of the department? I mean, with your incessant chatter and birdlike laughter.'

'Birdlike laughter?' She opened her mouth in mock indignation. 'Surely you jest, Harry. Tell me you're just tired and don't mean what you say.'

'There. Just like that. I bet I would have read about Weaver being taken away in a strait jacket.'

Alex laughed. 'He never called my laughter *bird-like*. That's all you.'

'Not to your face, anyway.'

'Oh, away with yourself. Stan often said he had never met anybody quite like me in his entire life.'

'I can pretty much say the same thing.' His phone rang and he took it out of his pocket. It was Weaver. 'McNeil,' Harry said, answering.

'Harry. I hope you don't mind but I need you to come down to the cemetery. I found something. I can't say on the phone.'

'Oh yeah? We were just heading out, but I can make it down there.'

'Oh, okay. But listen, there are things about that case that weren't right.'

'Like what?'

'Just some things that were said at the time.'

'Okay, I'll keep that in mind.' He paused for a moment. 'You been drinking, Stan?'

'What, are you my mother now? I have to answer to you? I don't think so. And you would do well to remember that. Just get your arse down here, McNeil.'

Harry disconnected the call. 'Uncle Stan isn't too happy with me.'

'You should have put it on speaker and I could have told him where to go.'

'You'll get to say it to his face; he wants us to go down to Warriston.'

'We were going there anyway.'

'I think he's still hungover. He must have forgot.'

Alex stared ahead through the windscreen. 'I don't care that he's retiring, Harry; I won't have him slag me off.' She looked at him. 'Or treat us like crap.'

The trailers had moved further down the site when they got there; closer to the old caretaker's house.

Alex pulled in behind Miller's car as it stopped and they saw the others getting out.

'You ready, sir?' Miller said to Harry. Purcell was standing nearby.

'Let's do it.'

'What's going on, sir?' Alex said.

'Come on. You should see this. And later, when you feel like lecturing me, this was a need-to-know basis.' He looked at Miller. 'Which one is Kline's trailer?'

'The one over the other side of that incline. We can't see it from here.'

'Are you going to arrest Kline?' Alex asked.

'Just come with us.'

Purcell took out his phone. 'You ready over there?' He waited for the answer before hanging up. 'Hazel

Carter is there with two of your team, McNeil. In case he makes a run for it.'

'Let's go,' Miller said, heading off round the hill.

Kline's trailer was sitting on its own. It was eerily silent. They approached as though they were just looking to sit down and have a cup of coffee.

Miller opened the door and he stepped inside, followed by Harry and Alex.

The two men inside turned round suddenly.

'What are you doing here, Miller?' Stan Weaver said. Charlie Meekle was standing next to him. They were both wearing leather gloves, despite it being warm outside. 'Did you bring them here, McNeil? I trusted you!'

'Shut up,' Harry said.

'Talk to a superior officer like that? I demand that you get out of here, Miller. You're impeding an investigation. And take that silly bitch with you.'

'They're here under my orders, Weaver.' Percy Purcell stepped through the door.

Weaver just stood looking at the other detectives.

'What's in the bag, Stan?' Harry said.

They all looked at the carrier bag Meekle was holding.

'None of your damn business.'

'Sorry, Stan, I can't do this anymore. It's killing me.' Meekle handed the bag to Miller. 'It's a pair of that lassie's knickers. I got them from Graham Balfour. He'd slept with her and she had left some stuff at his house. We were going to say we caught Kline stashing it.'

'Are you fucking daft?' Weaver said.

'It's over. They know or else they wouldn't be here.' The hard-bitten Glaswegian detective, who now looked pitiful, looked at Harry. 'I killed Jill Thompson. She was my stepdaughter.'

'Shut up, ya clown!' Weaver shouted. 'They know nothing.'

'Why do you think we're here, Weaver?' Purcell said. 'We have DNA results from that night. Taken from Jill. Go on, Meekle.'

'I had been drinking the night she died. A lot. We had a fight. She said she was going to the cemetery to meet her boyfriend. I followed her, but by Christ, I was staggering all over the place. I don't remember much about that night, but I remember catching up to her here, near the old house. We were arguing. It got heated. I tried to grab her arm but she scratched me. I remember falling and hitting my head on the gravestone. It must have toppled on top of her.' He looked at them all. 'I didn't mean to kill her. You have to believe me.'

Purcell nodded. 'I do believe you. When I said we have the results from the DNA test, I didn't mean we had skin samples from Jill's fingernails when she scratched you. I mean, we have the results from Jill's baby. We know who the father was.' He looked at Weaver.

'It's over for you now, Stan,' Harry said. 'We know you're the father.'

Meekle looked puzzled. 'What do you mean, Stan's the father?'

'You know as well as I do that every serving officer's DNA is on file, in case we have to eliminate them from a crime scene. We put Jill's baby's DNA through the system and we got a match; Stan Weaver was the father.'

'Is this true?' Meekle looked at Stan, and Harry thought he was about to take a swing at Weaver. He reached over and guided him away.

All the air seemed to go out of Weaver. 'It's true. You said Jill told you she was meeting her boyfriend that night, and she was: me.'

'Dirty bastard.'

'I was thirty-six back then. Not an old fart like now. I couldn't help it. You know yourself, she dressed and acted like a twenty-year-old, not fifteen. She knew what she was doing, let me tell you. Then, that night, she told me she was pregnant. My life, my career, would have been over.'

'You killed my daughter?' Meekle shook his head.

Weaver nodded. 'Yes. I was hiding. We saw you

coming in, shouting and staggering about. I didn't want a confrontation. I watched you fight with her and fall against the gravestone. But you didn't hit it hard enough to topple it. I saw that as my way out. I hit her and put her on the ground. Then I pushed it on top of her and then I took your mobile out of your pocket and called my number, making it look like you had called me. I waited fifteen minutes, then I slapped you and brought you round and you were begging me not to tell anybody. I convinced you that you had called me. I knew we in CID would get called out from Gayfield Square and I was right. We got the case. I was able to hide some stuff and make things disappear when they thought they were getting close, but I diverted their attention onto Graham Balfour. He was obviously never convicted.' He looked at Meekle. 'Sorry.'

'Bastard. I trusted you.'

Weaver looked at Harry. 'You're getting the cold case unit to yourself earlier than expected.'

'No, I'm not,' Harry said. 'I'm not working the cold case unit. I was brought in to investigate you. I was never going to be a part of the cold case unit. Yes, I'm almost finished with Professional Standards, but this was going to be my last case with them.'

Alex turned round and left the trailer without saying a word.

'You were investigating me? You little...'

'Why?' Meekle asked.

'When Trisha was murdered in the same way, we had a feeling that Weaver would somehow get himself involved in the case, to make sure things weren't going to lead back to him. We didn't know he had killed Jill twenty years ago, but there was certainly enough suspicion that he had been up to something. They drafted me in under the pretext I was taking over the cold case unit.'

'I didn't kill the Cornwall woman,' Weaver said.

'We know you didn't,' Miller said. 'Why did you try and put evidence in here?'

'To divert attention away from us. To make it look like Kline was the killer.'

'If Weaver didn't kill Trisha Cornwall, then who did?' Meekle asked.

THIRTY-EIGHT

Outside, Harry McNeil found Alex sitting on a gravestone that had been toppled years ago.

'Funny place to catch some rays,' he said to her as they were in the shadow of some trees.

She looked up at him. 'Why didn't you tell me?'

'I couldn't. Frank Miller and I were the only two who knew. It had to stay that way, especially since Commander Bridge asked Meekle to come up and give us some insight into the murders.'

'And you just left the two of them to their own devices.' She stood up and brushed off her jeans.

'We were hoping something would unravel. Weaver was a suspect right from the beginning. We hoped they would get together and try to make sure we didn't connect last week's murder to the one twenty years ago.'

She nodded. 'And they put you in place in such a short time?'

'Yes. As soon as Trisha Cornwall was found, this whole investigation was set up.'

'They don't mess about, do they?'

'Don't look so sad,' Harry said.

'Just when we thought we were getting rid of old grumpy and somebody half decent was taking over. I should have known it was too good to be true.'

'Look on the bright side; you still got rid of Weaver and there's no chance he'll be back. He's going to Saughton for murder.'

'Silver linings, eh?' She gave him a grim smile. 'I better get back to the office now that we're not needed.'

'I'll see you back there. I have to come back later.'

Alex walked away without turning back.

'What's going on in there?' Randy Kline said as he came towards the trailer.

'Mr Kline, nice timing.' Miller turned towards him.

'You didn't answer my question.'

'We're waiting for your son.'

'What do you want with Dustin?' Kline looked over into the distance. Saw his son walking between the gravestones. 'Dustin!'

All heads turned and they watched Dustin Crowd running. Miller and his team started running towards him.

Dustin jumped into the white caterer's van, started it up and took off. The caterer jumped out of his food trailer and started shouting. 'Where's he going with my van?'

Miller and Harry were about to jump into their cars when they saw an old Ford Focus pull in front of the van which collided with the passenger side and came to a halt.

They all ran towards the scene, Miller in the lead. He reached the van to find Dustin Crowd with a bleeding nose. Harry approached the Focus. The airbags in both vehicles had gone off.

Harry reached the Focus and pulled the driver's door open. 'Jesus, Alex, are you okay?'

She smiled at him, blood running down her face. 'No more smelly socks.'

THIRTY-NINE

Purcell watched the interview on the monitor from another room. Harry McNeil and Frank Miller were doing the interview in the room in the high street station. Dustin Crowd had been seen to by the force doctor and his nose had stopped bleeding. It wasn't broken.

Miller pushed the folder across towards Dustin's solicitor. 'The DNA results. From the piece of spandex that was pulled from your client's face.'

Dustin seemed to be staring into space for a moment. 'My dad had nothing to do with this. He wasn't involved.'

'You have the floor, Dustin,' Harry said. 'You can tell us in your own words why you killed those women, or you can just disappear into the ether. Nobody will know the story of why the great actor Dustin Crowd turned into a killer.'

'It wasn't like I was some nut job.'

'Tell us how it was, then,' Miller said.

Dustin paused, as if he was going to deliver some line. 'Trisha Cornwall was blackmailing my dad.'

'For the record, can you say who your father is?' Harry said.

'Randy Kline.'

'Fine. Carry on.'

'Trisha was blackmailing him. I overheard them one night, talking in the cemetery. Trisha was Jill Thompson's best friend, twenty years ago. She said that Jill confided in her, and that my dad was the father of her baby. She was fifteen! If it came out now that my dad had slept with a fifteen-year-old back then, his career would be over. Trisha was telling my dad that people would think he killed Jill because of the baby. She wanted more money. My dad said he would get it to her the following day. He left and that rancid cow was about to go as well. I hit her on the head with a real hammer we use for filming certain angles. Then I pushed the gravestone on top of her.'

'Did Kline, your father, see this?'

'No. He was on his way back to his trailer.'

'What about Aileen Rogers?'

'She was my make-up artist. I put latex on my face,

made myself up a bit. Put a beard on. You can actually make them look like they're real nowadays and I'd watched Aileen do it for many hours as she made me up. She didn't even suspect.'

'It's hard to believe she couldn't see right through it.'

'I met her when it was dark, I borrowed the catering van, made sure the lights didn't come on inside when we opened the door.'

'Why did you choose her?' Harry said.

'She was weak and vulnerable. We would talk when she was doing my make-up. She said she was going to leave her husband, and I suggested a chat room. She thought it was a good idea, and I gave her the website for one, and when I asked her if she joined, she told me her online name. I contacted her and gave her some spiel and we agreed to meet up. She didn't know it was me.'

'What happened after you got her into the cemetery?' Miller asked.

'I don't want you to think it was easy for me. I just told myself I was filming a scene, which I was going to do anyway, so this was like a rehearsal. I had to make it look like there was a killer on the loose. Physically, it was easy as I'd put a little something in the champagne we had.'

'And Rita Mellon?'

'Her boyfriend, that idiot who called himself Carruthers Wellington, had left his phone in the trailer one day. Rita called him. I saw her number and chose her. I sent her a text from a throwaway phone and said we should meet up for dinner so I could invest in the show. I told her Brian had given me the number. She fell for it. And I would have killed her if it wasn't for that guy with the dog.'

'And she clawed your face and got some of your mask. Which had your DNA on it because it was on your skin,' Harry said.

'The wonders of modern science.' Dustin sat back in the chair. 'I know what people are going to think of me, but I want them to know my father didn't harm anybody. He was innocent in all of this.'

'There is one thing,' Harry said. 'You said Trisha was blackmailing your dad, telling him he was the father of Jill's baby, twenty years ago.'

'Yes, I just told you that. Jill told Trisha back then that her boyfriend was my dad.'

'She was lying; we got the DNA results back and the father wasn't your dad. Randy Kline wasn't the father of Jill's baby. You killed her for nothing.'

The screams Dustin Crowd let out were better than any acting he had ever done.

'Jesus, he was pretending he was in a scene from his show?' Purcell said after Dustin Crowd had been taken down to the holding cells.

'It would seem that way. He doesn't have much grip on reality.'

Harry looked at his watch. 'If you'll excuse me, sir,' he said to Purcell, 'I have to get back to the office at HQ.'

'You did well there, McNeil. You both did.'

'Thank you.' Harry was walking away when Purcell stopped him.

'I'll see you soon.'

FORTY

Simon Gregg was arm wrestling DI Karen Shiels when Harry walked into the office at HQ.

'Bear in mind, I'll kick you in the balls if you hurt my arm,' she said to him.

Gregg let her win.

'Good job, sir,' he said to Harry.

'Thank you. It was a team effort. But we have an announcement to make.'

'Who's we?' Karen said.

'Me and DCI McNeil,' said Jeni Bridge, coming into the room. Alex was behind her, a white clip on her nose.

'It's just to help the air flow,' she said.

'DS Maxwell helped stop a killer. We lost a car in the process, but it needed to be replaced, by all accounts.' She sat down on a chair, indicating for everybody else to sit.

'DS Maxwell knows the story, but the rest of you don't. DCI McNeil wasn't here to take over the department from DCI Weaver; he was here to investigate him.'

A rumble of muttering started up and Jeni held up a hand. 'Sorry for keeping you in the dark, but it needed to be that way. However, I also have some more news for you; the cold case unit isn't going to exist in its present state, as of this week.

'Next Monday morning, this department will be staffed by civilians. Ex-detectives, under the leadership of George Carr and Willie Young, who are doing a sterling job. The chief constable and the police board decided that the detectives here were wasting their talent. Or we were wasting valuable resources, whatever way you want to look at it. Cutbacks are happening all over Scotland. So, here's what we came up with, DCI McNeil is going to head up a third MIT unit. God knows there's enough work for us. However, there are smaller police areas that don't benefit from having the resources or the need for a full-time MIT unit, so this third team will go and assist in certain areas of the country.'

'What's going to happen to us?' Alex asked.

'There's a position for you all in the new team. If

you want it. You will work under DCI McNeil, who reports to me and directly to Superintendent Purcell. Would you like to move to the new unit? It will still be based here in the HQ building.'

Alex, Gregg, and Karen all said they would be very happy to move.

'Great. First thing Monday morning, nice and sharp. You are all officially off the cold case unit.'

Jeni got up and left the room.

'You're not getting rid of me that easily,' Harry said.

Alex laughed. 'Jesus, that hurts.'

'Let's just hope they get us better cars,' Harry said. 'Or maybe not. What with the way you drive. Pulling out in front of a van like that...'

FORTY-ONE

Peter Hanson paid the taxi driver and waited for his change. 'I don't get a tip at my work!' he shouted to the back of the cab as it drove away. Then he stumbled up the pathway to his front door. To the house that Frank Miller didn't know about.

'Tell me I'm not already a better detective than he is,' he said out loud, fumbling with his key. Finally, he got it into the lock and went inside.

Then he stopped. He thought he'd heard a noise inside. Was it Steffi? No. She didn't know about this place; his bachelor pad before he'd met his wife.

Nobody knew about this place.

He gently closed the door and walked along the hallway, staggering a few times. He'd left a lamp on a timer and it was switched on.

There were two people in his living room. Women.

What the hell was going on?

'What do you think you're doing?' he said.

One of the women turned to him and smiled. 'We're waiting for you.'

'What?'

'We wanted to have a talk with you,' the other said.

'That will be right. Get the hell out of my house.'

Then he felt a push in his back from somebody behind him and he went flying into the room, landing face down on the carpet. He looked round from the floor and saw a big man framed in the doorway.

'Who are you?' he said.

'Never mind who I am, Peter. It's who I represent you should be worried about. My boss wanted us to give you a wee message.'

One of the women kicked him hard in the stomach while the other pulled his hair and punched him in the face.

'I'm going to kick your spleen out, you bitches,' Hanson yelled, trying to get up.

The man stepped forward. 'These two women know more ways to inflict pain than you've had hot showers. We're going to take you somewhere, to a place where you will be taught a lesson.'

'Did Steffi put you up to this? Are you a bunch of coppers who think this is funny? Well, I'll show her. She won't fuck with me again.'

'Oh, you're right on that count; she will most definitely not fuck with you ever again.'

The man walked over and crouched down to him. 'The police couldn't find you. You made yourself disappear; no mobile phone use, no cash machine use, no nothing. They think you're on the run. They don't know about this place because you kept it on without telling anybody about it. In other words, you've already made our job easy. You've disappeared and nobody knows where you are.'

'How did you find me?'

'Simple. When you applied for the police, this was the address you used.'

He took out a syringe and stuck it into Hanson's neck, then he stood up.

Anybody who saw him coming home drunk would just see him coming back out drunk, only this time with three friends. Like they were celebrating.

Outside, the two women acted like they were having a good time and holding their friend Peter up.

The black van pulled up outside the tenement building. This part of Leith was quiet at this time of night. The side door slid open and Hanson was shoved inside. The women got in after him. The man climbed in beside the driver.

Peter Hanson would never lift his hand to a woman ever again.

AFTERWORD

Thank you for reading this Frank Miller and I hope you enjoyed Harry McNeil.

A usual, I would like to thank the following people for their support – Louise Unsworth Murphy, Wendy Haines, Julie Stott, Fiona and Adrian Jackson, Jeni Bridge, Michelle Barragan, Evelyn Bell, Merrill Astill Blount, Vanessa Kerrs, Bejay Roles and Barbara Bartley.

Thank you to my wife Debbie, and my daughters, Stephanie and Samantha.

And a big thank you to Melanie Underwood.

I would also like to address the issue of domestic violence.

My mother was a retired police officer and a

widow, when she would have a drink with some friends at her local bar. There, she met a very charming and likeable man. They started dating and he treated her like a lady. Until one night when he'd had one too many. Then she met the real man. He hit her. And then he was full of apologies, it would never happen again, he asked for another chance. Which he got. And that opened the gate. He hit her again, and despite the promises, he did it again. Until enough was enough. She told him to go, they were finished. But he wasn't finished. He broke into her house one night to cause her harm, but luckily, she wasn't home. He left her a note saying what he was going to do to her.

I wish she had gone to the police, but she told me, "I was a police officer. I've helped victims of domestic violence. It shouldn't have happened to me. I should have called it a day after the first time he hit me." She ended up selling her house and moving and she never had contact with the man again.

I was furious, and was only told about this after the fact. Only then did I understand why she moved so quickly.

I was unable to do anything to help her then because I didn't know it was going on. My mother got a lucky escape and went on to enjoy the rest of her retirement before passing away from breast cancer.

If you – man or woman – find yourself in such a

situation, please try and find help. It is easier said than done, I know, but please try. My mother was one of the lucky ones. No person ever has the right to lift their hands to their significant other.

John Carson
New York
December 2019

ABOUT THE AUTHOR

John Carson is originally from Edinburgh but now lives with his wife and family in New York State. And two dogs. And four cats. Sometimes he manages to squeeze some writing time in.

website - johncarsonauthor.com

Facebook - JohnCarsonAuthor

Twitter - JohnCarsonBooks

Instagram - JohnCarsonAuthor